'Warm,' said the Dream Master, whose own face was turning red, 'is an understatement. It's blistering hot, and yet – 'he gazed up at the sky – 'there's no sun, so where is the heat coming from?'

Cy glanced at his feet. 'There seems to be steam coming out of the ground.'

The Dream Master looked down. A few metres from where they stood a trickle of orange fluid was oozing towards them. 'Lava!' he shrieked.

'Funny, warm and clever these books provide informative and thought-provoking entertainment'
Guardian

'An entertaining and deceptively informative fantasy adventure' *Scotsman*

DREAM MASTER

GLADIATOR

THERESA BRESLIN

Illustrated by David Wyatt

CORGI YEARLING BOOKS

DREAM MASTER: GLADIATOR
A CORGI YEARLING BOOK 0 440 86501 8

First published in Great Britain by Doubleday,
an imprint of Random House Children's Books

Doubleday edition published 2003
Corgi Yearling edition published 2004

1 3 5 7 9 10 8 6 4 2

Corgi Books are published by Random House Children's Books,
61–63 Uxbridge Road, London W5 5SA,
a division of The Random House Group Ltd,
in Australia by Random House Australia (Pty) Ltd,
20 Alfred Street, Milsons Point, Sydney, NSW 2061, Australia,
in New Zealand by Random House New Zealand Ltd,
18 Poland Road, Glenfield, Auckland 10, New Zealand,
and in South Africa by Random House (Pty) Ltd,
Endulini, 5A Jubilee Road, Parktown 2193, South Africa

THE RANDOM HOUSE GROUP Limited Reg. No. 954009
www.kidsatrandomhouse.co.uk

A CIP catalogue record for this book is available from the British Library.

Printed and bound in Great Britain by
Cox & Wyman Ltd, Reading, Berkshire

This book is for David and Alice in
far-off Maniototo

Every
dream must
have a Dream
Master – to keep the
dream in order. My
dreamcloak helps me move
through Time and Space to
give you the dream that you
want. But sometimes, someone
with a really vivid imagination
gets inside their own dream.
That's when there can be Trouble...

CHAPTER I

'K now anything about volcanoes?'

Cy stopped rummaging through his bookcase and turned to speak to the small worried-looking dwarf who was sitting cross-legged on his bed arranging the folds of a large silky cloak.

'Dream Master,' Cy said in a louder voice. 'I need some fast facts about a famous volcano.'

The little man didn't raise his head. 'Etna, Olympus Mons, Krakatoa, Mount St Helens. Which?'

'All. Any,' said Cy. He stepped aside smartly as a pile of books cascaded onto his bedroom floor. 'School starts soon and I've got to hand in an assignment about volcanoes to Mrs Chalmers.'

The Dream Master glanced up. 'The week before a major school project is due to be handed in is *not* the time to be researching the subject.'

'What do you suggest then?' asked Cy. 'The week after?'

Cy's Dream Master looked at him severely. 'You have had all six weeks of the summer break to prepare your work for the new term. You shouldn't leave things until the last minute and then expect other people to do your homework for you.'

'It's not my fault. Our computer is on the blink and I couldn't look on the Internet,' said Cy. 'Are you going to help or not?'

'What do you want me to do?' said the little man crossly. 'Use my dreamcloak to take you on a volcano tour round the Pacific Ring of Fire? Volcanoes are extremely dangerous,' he went on quickly as Cy opened his mouth to say 'yes'. 'You don't want to be anywhere near one when it erupts.'

'Well, what about, sort of . . . close by?' asked Cy.

'Volatile Vulcan!' snapped the Dream Master. 'When Krakatoa blew up, the explosion was heard nearly *three thousand* miles away. It caused a huge tsunami tidal wave which washed up in Australia. Where volcanoes are concerned, "close by" is not an option.'

'Oh, all right,' said Cy in a calming tone of voice, 'an extinct one will do.' And then, as the Dream Master didn't reply, Cy pleaded, 'Can't you just hold up your dreamcloak and let me have a quick peek through it? If we both concentrate our minds on volcanoes we're bound to see something.'

The Dream Master hesitated.

'I'll be very careful only to think about *non*-active ones.' Cy knew that his Dream Master often complained that Cy let his Imagination run away with him when he was in his Dreamworld. He grabbed a notebook and pencil from his desk, and quickly wrote down the four volcanoes the Dream Master had mentioned. 'Look, I'll take notes. It will be my own work . . . mostly.'

'The problem is –' the Dream Master pulled out one of the folds of his dreamcloak – 'the problem is that a "quick peek" might not be an option either. Look at the state of this!'

'What?' Cy shoved his notebook in his pocket and sat down beside the little man. He looked at the part of the dreamcloak which the Dream

Master had spread out on his bed. The pattern of Cy's duvet cover shone clearly through the pale flowing ripples. 'I don't see anything.'

'Exactly,' said the Dream Master. 'You and your wild dreams are wearing me and my dreamcloak to a frazzle. If it's not Vikings from Valhalla, it's Extinct Egyptians. Every time I let you have a hand in your own dreams I end up doing Double Time to keep you out of Danger. Why can't you be like most other twenty-first-century humans who go to sleep and let their Dream Master order their dreams? *They* are quite happy with having *their* dreams inside their head. That's how it is supposed to happen, that's how humans dream. Why do I have the Incredible Ill Luck to be Dream Master to a stroppy boy who always wants to do it in reverse?' he added bitterly.

Cy didn't like to say that his dreams were *much* better when he managed to get inside his dream and dream up his own stories, rather than have his dream inside his head with the Dream Master doing the dreaming for him. So instead he said, 'My dreams are *interesting*. You said so yourself. You told me that ever since you let me have a say in thinking up the story of my own dreams your life had become more exciting.'

The Dream Master passed his hand across his face. '"Exciting" is not always pleasant. Do you know what the *pejorative* use of a word means? Never mind –' he held up his hand as Cy shook his head – 'you can look it up later. At my time of life one can have too much excitement. My dream-cloak is getting thin. I think your Imagination is wearing it out.'

Cy looked at the dreamcloak spilling out over his bed. Parts of it were almost like clear glass. Usually it was dark and deep, with currents flowing through the folds and hollows. If a dream was about to start, the cloak would thrum like wind through telephone wires. But now it lay passive and still. 'Isn't there any way to repair it?' he asked.

'I'm not sure,' said Cy's Dream Master, chewing on his beard. 'It's the first time I've ever seen it look so shallow and pale. There is an unsteady, dangerous feel all around it, and . . .' He hesitated.

'And what?'

'Well, look here.' The Dream Master pointed to the hem of his dreamcloak. 'Do you remember at the end of the Egyptian dream when a bit of my cloak got torn off?'

'Yes,' said Cy. 'When we left the Valley of the

Kings I was holding onto the dreamcloak so tightly that part of it came away in my hand. What about it?'

'Well, the part of the cloak where the piece was torn off has faded away completely. It's invisible, as if . . . as if . . . my dreamcloak is leaking.'

'*Leaking?*' said Cy. 'Leaking what?'

'Whatever energy it's made of,' the Dream Master said crossly.

'What *is* it made of?' asked Cy.

'It's too difficult to explain to you,' said the Dream Master quickly. 'You are too young and too . . . too . . . *human* to understand.'

Cy groaned. Adults always did this if they couldn't be bothered to explain something, or if they didn't want to admit that they didn't really know about it themselves. Nearly every adult, that is, except his grampa, who always said that 'understanding relies on things being properly explained.'

'My grampa,' began Cy, 'says that understanding relies on—'

'Anyway, at the moment it doesn't matter what energy it is made of,' the Dream Master interrupted rudely. 'What I'm concerned about is where my dreamcloak's energy is going.'

'Maybe we should have tried to stitch that torn piece back on?' suggested Cy.

The Dream Master gave Cy a filthy look. 'Puh-*lease*! Who do you think I am? Peter Pan?'

Cy jumped off the bed and, kneeling down, he carefully pulled out the bottom drawer of his chest of drawers. In the space below were his precious things, hidden away from his nosy older sister Lauren. He pushed aside his fossil stone, Grampa's war medal and the little matchbox with the sand from Arabia. There, nestling below them, was the scrap of dreamsilk torn from the Dream Master's cloak. It was strange how sometimes it could move like quicksilver, yet just now it appeared to be slumbering. As if it were resting. And yet it gave the appearance of not being completely still. It looked, Cy thought, more as if it were *waiting* . . . So innocent but so powerful, holding every potential dream that he might have.

Cy knew that he had to be very, very careful about what he was thinking of whenever he touched the dreamsilk. His Dream Master had warned him many times: 'Remember, in a dream you can have all that the Imagination allows. Anything can happen – anything at all.' Keeping his mind focused only on the dreamsilk, Cy gently lifted out the piece of dark material. It looked different somehow, but he didn't know in what way. As he held it out to show the Dream Master the edges drifted down over his hand. 'Can't we reconnect it to the main part of the cloak? This torn piece looks in better condition, as if it has more energy. It might help re-energize the dreamcloak.'

'It might also ignite a chain reaction of unknown power.' The Dream Master stretched out his hand to pick it up. And then he stopped, his fingers a millimetre away from touching the dreamsilk. He peered closely at the scrap of material in Cy's hand.

'Suffering Stromboli,' he whispered.

'What is it?' asked Cy, suddenly conscious that the scrap of silk had turned warm in his hand.

'I see Trouble,' said the Dream Master.

'Twenty Types of Trouble – Double Mixed?' asked Cy.

'Much worse,' said the Dream Master. 'This is Triple Trouble.' He gave Cy a look of absolute terror. 'Triple Trouble Times Ten.'

'Triple Trouble Times Ten ...' Cy repeated slowly.

When faced with a problem Cy's brain always slowed down. Inside his head he heard gears clunking, grinding together like an old car with a clapped-out engine. He wished his friend Vicky was here. She was great at mental arithmetic.

'Triple Trouble. . .' he muttered under his breath. 'Triple . . . That's three threes . . . and three times three times three is—'

'A lot,' snapped the Dream Master. 'Don't you see how that piece of dreamsilk has changed? How it has *grown*?'

Of course! Cy now saw what was different about his piece of dreamcloak since the last time he had seen it. The torn section had once fitted into the palm of his hand. Now it was overlapping the edges, trailing over his fingers. And as he gazed at it he felt it start to vibrate gently. Hurriedly he laid it on the bed.

'Look!' wailed the Dream Master, holding up the frayed hem of his dreamcloak. '*My* dreamcloak is tattered at the end. *Your* piece is growing stronger.'

'Omigosh!' gasped Cy.

The Dream Master was right. Under Cy's gaze the small piece of dreamsilk glowed red. And it was moving. In contrast to the Dream Master's own cloak, which lay inert on Cy's bed. Cy glanced up. The day was warm, his bedroom window was open, but there was no wind. Yet the silk shimmered with life. Cy reached out his hand.

'*Don't touch it!*' shrieked the Dream Master, grabbing at Cy's arm to snatch him back.

Too late.

As Cy's fingers connected, there was a blinding crack, a roar of hot rushing air, and Cy and his Dream Master were sucked inside the whirlpool of TimeSpace.

CHAPTER II

Cy fell into Time and Space. A racing swirl of tumbled thoughts and emotions engulfed him. Concentrations of silent dark streaming energy raced past him as he accelerated through dimensions of Hope, Joy, Grief ... and Fear. Cy trembled as Fear reached out to him. He gasped as an icy shiver of terror tried to pin itself to his mind. He twisted away and began to fall further and faster.

'This is all wrong!' cried the Dream Master.

Cy felt fear again. The Dream Master was right.

Things weren't happening as they should. It *was* all wrong, but Cy did not know why. In previous dreams, Time and Space would move in a more *ordered* way. This was a scary jumbled chaos.

From far away Cy heard the Dream Master yell, 'Concentrate! Cy, concentrate!'

Everything was going too fast. Cy gripped his piece of dreamsilk. What had he been thinking back there in his bedroom? He would have to focus quickly or . . .

A gap of light appeared in the darkness. There was a loud bang; Cy and the Dream Master collided, and then nose-dived through a gap in TimeSpace, landing in a heap together.

'Where are we?' asked Cy, struggling to his feet.

'That is *such* a cliché,' said the Dream Master.

Cy ignored him. The little man was always more crabby than usual when things happened unexpectedly. Cy looked around him. He was standing among boulders and stones. 'I think we're on a hill of some kind,' said Cy. Mist and fog-like vapour were preventing him from seeing very far. 'It could be a mountain slope.'

'You think?' The Dream Master was having difficulty standing up on the rocky terrain. 'You *think*? You are supposed to *know*.' He pointed to the piece of dreamsilk still clutched in Cy's hand. 'It is *your* dream. Therefore you *know*.' He peered through the fog. 'Does this mountain have a name?'

'I'm not very good at remembering names,' said Cy.

The Dream Master turned a piercing gaze on Cy. 'It shouldn't be a case of you *remembering*,' he said. 'You should *know* the name of the mountain we are standing on. We can't arrive anywhere in a dream without the dream's Dream Master dreaming it up first.'

Cy was beginning to feel uncomfortably warm and it wasn't just because the Dream Master was asking him questions that he couldn't answer. 'Well,' he said, pushing his sleeves up, 'it's a *warm* mountain. I know that at least.'

'Warm,' said the Dream Master, whose own face was turning red, 'is an understatement. It's blistering hot, and yet –' he gazed up at the sky – 'there's no sun, so where is the heat coming from?'

Cy glanced at his feet. 'There seems to be steam coming out of the ground.'

The Dream Master looked down. A few metres from where they stood a trickle of orange fluid was oozing towards them. 'Lava!' he shrieked. 'Red hot lava! You promised me that you would only want to see extinct volcanoes!'

'Actually,' said Cy, 'I haven't thought of *any* volcanoes.'

'Well, what *have* you been thinking of?' demanded the Dream Master. 'You were holding your piece of dreamcloak when this happened. There must have been something in your mind that brought us here.'

Cy thought for a moment, then shook his head. 'Er, nothing.'

'That's impossible,' snorted the Dream Master. 'You can't just think of *nothing*!' He rolled his eyes in his head. 'Why is it,' he fumed, 'that when trying to organize a dream, I always get the Idiotic Imbecilic Ignoramus whose Imagination is—'

'Hold on a minute,' said Cy. '*You're* the one who has been teaching *me* mind-control so that I can guide my dreams more carefully. How to take pauses, how to be slow to rise to anger, how to quieten anxiety.' In fact, Cy thought, it was very like the advice that his grampa gave him to ward off the panic attacks which swamped him if too many things happened too quickly. 'Try taking your own advice.' Cy stood in front of the Dream Master and spoke to him firmly. 'Calm down.'

'I am doing my best,' said the Dream Master. 'It is not easy.' He took a deep breath. 'You are a particularly . . . challenging . . . pupil.'

'Perhaps,' Cy persisted, 'but example is the best teacher. You should *show* me how to behave. I don't ever notice you being very patient.'

'When you are an expert, as I am,' said the Dream Master, 'you don't need so much patience.'

'If you are such an expert,' said Cy, 'then *you* get us out of here.'

The Dream Master swung his arm round behind him to scoop up the great folds of his own dreamcloak . . . and grasped empty air.

'What is it?' Cy asked. His voice faltered as he saw the look of stunned disbelief on his Dream Master's face.

'I don't have it.' The Dream Master began to bite his beard in fury. 'You Blithering Bumbling Bungling Boy!' he roared. 'My dreamcloak! My precious dreamcloak! It's still lying on your bed!'

'Omigosh,' said Cy.

The Dream Master stamped his foot in fury and then grabbed his toes and began hopping around on one foot. 'Ouch! Ouch! I've burned myself!'

'Try not to get stressed,' said Cy, with more

confidence than he actually felt. 'I'm sure we can move on from this place—'

There was an almighty crash. Cy and the Dream Master were scooped up in an explosion of energy. TimeSpace expanded and contracted like a gigantic rubber band. They catapulted forwards and stopped abruptly, teetering on the edge of a giant crater.

'This looks better.' Cy pulled out his notebook and began to scribble. 'It's definitely extinct, and it's a lot cooler.'

'Cooler!' repeated the Dream Master irritably. 'It's freezing! Hurry up and take your notes and let's get out of here.' He peered into the vast empty hole. 'Where is "here" exactly?'

Cy didn't answer.

'You still don't know! Look, Cy,' the Dream Master said seriously, 'it's unsafe to travel through TimeSpace in this way. You do understand that it is a bit like a story? We must have *some* order to where we are going.'

'Order,' repeated Cy. He glanced at his notebook. And then he saw the names of the volcanoes that the Dream Master had told him earlier. 'I get it now!'

The Dream Master understood almost at the same moment Cy did. 'We are visiting the volcanoes in the order you wrote them down! The first, with the lava flow, was Etna in Sicily. It is still active. Now we are at Olympus Mons on Mars. That's why it is so cold!'

'And the next one is Krakatoa.'

Cy had barely finished his sentence when he and his Dream Master tumbled with a great *felump!* onto the bottom of a tiny boat.

'Not the South China Sea!' moaned the Dream Master.

'Is that near Krakatoa?' asked Cy.

'We don't *want* to be near Krakatoa,' said the Dream Master. 'The tidal wave? Remember?'

Cy looked again at his notebook and began to read aloud: 'Etna, Olympus Mons, Krakatoa, Mount St He—'

The Dream Master grabbed the notebook from Cy's hand. 'Don't say it!' he screamed. *'DON'T EVEN THINK IT!* That last one on your list is the most dangerous of all. If you'd studied your subject at all over the summer holidays you'd know that the force which blew the top off that mountain was equal to over a thousand nuclear bombs. The pyroclastic surge which followed scorched the whole area for miles and miles. If we go anywhere near that one we're both goners.'

CHAPTER III

'an I stop us going there?' asked Cy.
'Of course you can. It's your dream.' The
Dream Master spoke slowly and distinctly.
'But you will need – to – concentrate – very – care-
fully – indeed.'

A part of Cy's brain registered that the little man
was speaking to him in the same way that some
adults address the very old, the very young, or the
very mad. He's scared, thought Cy. He is really scared
at what I might do. He is so terrified, in fact, that
for the first time ever he has stopped shouting at me.

'I need help,' Cy whispered.

The Dream Master gripped his arm. 'Think of some other volcano,' he said in an encouraging voice.

'I can't.' As always, when in a tricky situation, Cy's brain had slipped to the bottom of his head.

'San Francisco?' suggested the Dream Master. 'Didn't something happen in California at the beginning of the twentieth century when San Francisco nearly burned down?'

'That was an *earthquake*,' said Cy. 'We don't do earthquakes until after we've done volcanoes.'

'Excuse *me*!' said the Dream Master. 'I'm sorry I've not kept up to date with the changes in the school curriculum.'

'Don't worry about it. Nobody can,' said Cy. 'You should hear my mum about how little attention is given to her modern languages department, but that's not the point anyway.'

'Ten out of ten, Cy!' The Dream Master spoke through gritted teeth. His face was contorted with the effort of trying to keep his temper. 'You are absolutely correct. That is *not* the point.'

Cy gave himself a shake. There had to be some kind of safe thought in his head ... something comforting ...

Suddenly from nowhere there was a blur in the air above the raft.

The Dream Master waved his arms. 'What is going on? What is flying about up there?'

'It's Peter!' said Cy. 'It's Peter Pan!'

'I can't stand it!' shrieked the Dream Master. 'At this moment in Time you must *not* get involved in a dream where myth gets mythed— mixed up.' He pointed upwards. 'Get rid of him. He can't help us in this situation.'

Cy felt that familiar panicky feeling when things happened too fast for him to cope with. It would sometimes happen in class if he had to read aloud. Mrs Chalmers usually gave him time to gather his thoughts but even she could be impatient. 'Why can't I think of anything fast or quickly enough?' he moaned. 'It's always like this with me. My brain doesn't work at speed, especially when I'm under pressure.'

'Stop whining,' snapped the Dream Master, 'and think of something relevant to the situation.'

'I'm trying to think of something. I must have thought of Peter Pan, but that was to do with you having your cloak sewn back together.' Cy turned to the Dream Master. 'Why didn't that work then? Why didn't we move on to a dream about Peter Pan?'

'Don't be a Dimwit,' screeched the Dream Master, beginning to lose it again. 'Haven't you learned *anything* in all the dreams you've done previously? There's got to be a link.'

'A link?' Cy repeated.

'Yes,' said the Dream Master impatiently. 'Think of story sequencing, think of continuity. You can't just jump randomly from one topic to another unless you establish a link.'

'What's that then?' asked Cy.

'*Transition!*' yelled the Dream Master. 'The change or passage from one state or stage to another. Find a way to move from one scene to the next without losing control of the story – or, in your case, the dream.'

'Uh.' Cy stared through the blurring rain that had begun to fall. The wind was rising and the swell of the sea started to buffet their little boat.

'Didn't you do any research at all?' the Dream Master yelled at Cy.

'Of course I did,' Cy shouted back.

'Well, try and remember some of it. Find a link to get us out of here.'

Myths . . . The Dream Master's voice echoed in Cy's head. He had said something about myths. In times gone past it was how people explained happenings that they couldn't understand. That was where a lot of the old stories and legends came from, mankind trying to make sense of things for which they hadn't enough scientific knowledge. Anything violent in nature, they would say that the gods were angry. The Japanese thought that a volcano was a giant catfish moving underwater . . .

The boat heaved. A few miles away the ocean began to boil. Breaking the surface of the waves was a huge fin.

The Dream Master put his head in his hands. 'I can't look,' he moaned. 'Now we're going to be eaten by a catfish. Cy,' he said urgently, '*now* would be the best time for you to focus that thought. Cy!' he yelled as the boat began to up-end itself. 'Cy! Cy!'

'Cy . . .' Cy repeated his own name. 'Cy . . .' He searched in his mind for any piece of information which might help him out of this fix. '. . . clops,' he finished, and grinned wildly at the Dream Master.

'Clops?' The Dream Master gave him a baffled look.

'Transition!' cried Cy. 'I've done it! In Italy some-where there's an extinct volcano. I read about it in one of my books. From a distance the crater looks like a giant eye. In ancient times it was thought to be the one-eyed giants who helped the fire god in his underground forge. They were called the Cyclops who fought with fire and rocks.'

The Dream Master spread apart his fingers and peered at Cy with one eye. 'Cy ... cyclops?' he said.

'Yep,' said Cy.

'Is that the best transition you can do?'

'It's a good one,' said Cy. 'Vesuvius was a volcano but it hasn't erupted for quite a while.'

'And we hope never again,' said a soft voice at Cy's elbow.

Cy turned. He was among vineyards on a sunny hillside. A young woman stood beside him.

'Although –' she looked upwards – 'the sky has been cloudy, which is unseasonal for this time of year, and there is a strange breeze blowing offshore. Like this.' And she blew softly into Cy's face.

'That's not how you wake someone up,' said a kind voice. 'Wake up, Cy. Wake up.'

'Wendy?' said Cy. He blinked, and looked at the figure standing between him and the light from his bedroom window. It *was* Wendy! She must have come to sew on Peter Pan's shadow. Great, thought Cy, she can mend the dreamcloak at the same time.

But she only laughed when Cy told her this. 'I don't think so,' she said. 'This afternoon you and I are going shopping.'

'Mum!' yelped Cy.

'You've been dreaming,' said Cy's mum. 'Come on, school starts next week. It's time to get you a new uniform.'

Cy sat up on his bed. 'Please no. I'm very busy today. I've got a school project to do.'

'We *have* to shop for new school clothes,' replied his mum. 'I don't enjoy it any more than you do. Don't make a fuss,' she begged. 'I've already had Lauren moaning at me and we haven't even started yet.'

'Can't you just buy the stuff and I'll wear it?' pleaded Cy. 'You know I don't care what it looks like. I'll wear anything.'

'No deal, Cy,' said his mum. 'It saves time if you come along. Then I know that we've got the right size.'

'It doesn't save *my* time,' Cy grumbled as he stood up. This was going to be an afternoon of torture. Lauren and his mother would now have pitched battles in every store in town, and still not agree on what was suitable school wear. For that to happen would require a peace commission more

30

powerful than for any war-torn country.

'I'd like you to be downstairs ready to leave in ten minutes, please.' Cy's mum stopped on her way out the door. 'There's a burning smell in here. You've not been playing about with matches, Cy, have you?' She looked at him closely.

'No!' said Cy.

His mum went to the window. 'Oh, it's Mr Bridges next door. He's got a bonfire blazing away there. It's such an end-of-the-summer smell, isn't it? Some smoke seems to have drifted in,' she said, wiping the soot marks off the window-ledge with her fingers. 'I wonder what he's burning?' She wrinkled her nose. 'It's got a very strong smell.'

Dragging his feet, Cy began to follow his mother out of the room. Then he too stopped and sniffed the air. His mum was right. There *was* an odd smell in his room. But it wasn't the smoke from their neighbour's bonfire.

The smell was like sulphur, he was sure of it. The type of smell you got from rotten eggs . . . the same kind of smell that hung around a volcano when it was about to erupt.

CHAPTER IV

'That skirt is *way* too short.'

In the girls' clothes department Cy's mum and his sister Lauren were in a fashion stand-off.

''Tisn't,' said Lauren. She hauled on the hemline of the micro Lycra skirt which clung to the top of her legs. Then she flounced back into the changing room and dragged the curtain closed.

'Lauren, come back out here!' cried Cy's mum. She opened her mouth to speak to Lauren again and then stopped. 'Remember the Communications

Course,' Cy heard her mutter under her breath. 'Give yourself time to gather your thoughts. Breathe deliberately. In through the nose and out through the mouth.' Cy's mum took a deep breath in, then she let air out of her mouth very carefully. 'Slowly, slowly. Now . . .' She contorted her face into an artificial smile. 'Lauren, dear,' she said in a jolly voice. '*Do* come back out and let me have another look at your new school skirt. Please,' she added quickly.

Cy hated it. He hated shopping. He particularly hated shopping for clothes. And he especially particularly hated shopping with his sister. Lauren and his mum clashed on every item. When Cy had to get geared up for school he usually chose the path of least resistance. Unless his mum was trying some awful outrage he just stood about, like today, raising and lowering his arms while she held trousers against his waist and jumpers across his shoulders. When he was forced to try something on he did so as fast as he possibly could and avoided looking in any mirrors. Whereas his older sister Lauren fought action on all fronts. School rucksack, skirt, shirt, pullover, shoes, the lot. She conceded nothing.

Once, when Cy's mum had been unwell, Lauren

had been given enough money to go shopping for all the items needed for her return to school in the autumn term. After a nine-hour shopping trip with her friends she had wandered home with one item, a designer-label jacket.

Cy's mum had gone pale. 'You were supposed to get two skirts, a pullover, shoes and some other things as well.'

'You don't really expect me to wear clothes that are cheap and nasty,' Lauren protested.

'With that amount of money I could have fed a family of four for a week,' shouted Cy's dad.

'We *are* a family of four,' Lauren said immediately. 'And can I remind you that your attempts to do just that on the evenings that you cook dinner are a trifle pathetic.'

'What?' Cy's dad's mouth dropped open.

'Oh, Lauren, that's unfair.' Cy's mum glanced anxiously at Cy's dad. 'Your meals are ... um ... lovely, darling.'

'Don't take it from me. Ask anybody.' Lauren flapped her hand about, then swiftly gathered up her shopping and left the room.

'I've never heard anyone complain.' Cy's dad turned to him. 'Is there anything wrong with the meals I prepare?'

'Cool.' Cy shrugged casually. He'd always found that a good way of getting out of tricky situations. And he'd perfected his shrug so that it was neither a yes nor a no. 'Cool,' he said again, and slid unobtrusively towards the door.

'Is my cooking in some way defective?' his dad repeated.

'Not at all, dear,' Cy heard his mum say soothingly as he went upstairs.

Later from his room Cy could hear his parents still talking, while in the bathroom Lauren hummed to herself as she washed her hair.

Now, Lauren reappeared from the changing room, and stood in front of her mother.

'Um.' Cy's mum called the sales girl over. 'Do you have this skirt in a slightly longer length?'

The sales assistant rolled her eyes. ''Slongest we've got.'

Lauren and the sales assistant exchanged glances over Cy's mum's head.

'Don't make them any longer'n that,' added the sales assistant. She put her head on one side. ''Sfine, s'far's I can see.'

Lauren shot her a grateful look.

Cy's mum swallowed. 'I think it's very short,' she said weakly.

Cy closed his eyes. It always followed the same pattern. He wished that he was anywhere else but in the girls' clothing section of a department store. He slid his hand into the pocket of his sweatshirt. His fingers connected with the piece of dreamsilk. Exactly *where* had he been with the Dream Master earlier on?

'The skirt is far too long.' An older woman's voice spoke firmly. 'My daughter must have her hemline shorter.'

Cy blinked.

'Mother,' replied an equally firm, but more youthful voice. 'This longer length is how I want to wear my clothes now.'

Cy blinked again. What had happened? One minute his mum was insisting that Lauren's skirt should be longer, and now she was taking the exact opposite point of view. Cy opened his eyes wide, and as he did so his mind made a strange little blip and then settled.

Around Cy everything had changed. From a brightly lit twenty-first-century department store he had flitted in TimeSpace to . . . where?

He was in a shop. But this shop was stacked from floor to ceiling with cloth. Cloth in bales, in rolls, hanging from the walls and the ceiling. And such different colours, and types of material. Deep indigo, stripes, silks and cotton. Cy peered round one of the bales of cloth. In place of his mum and his sister Lauren there were now two completely different people having a similar heated discussion. The girl had wrapped a piece of dark purple material about her waist while her mother sat on a low bench viewing her. A man with a goatee beard who seemed to be the shop owner was holding several other bolts of cloth under his arm.

'Look,' the girl appealed to the shopkeeper. 'Isn't there a certain grace as the folds of the cloth fall to the ground?'

'Indeed. Indeed.' The man bowed his head. 'The Tyrian-purple is most becoming.'

'I think it needs to be considerably shorter,' said the girl's mother. 'The streets are dusty in the summer heat and the cobbles become wet in winter. It is better to have the garment swing free.'

'I could gather it up with a belt,' said the girl.

'Then, Rhea Silvia, you would look like the matron Celia Andinus,' said the older woman. She turned to the shopkeeper. 'Would she not, Master Darius?'

'Indeed,' said the merchant. He looked from mother to daughter and kept his face impassive. 'Indeed,' he repeated.

'He will tell them that which they wish to hear in order to make a sale,' whispered a voice close to Cy.

Cy jumped and turned. There was a boy, younger than himself, sitting right beside him. He had a piece of yellowy paper in his hand and was drawing on it with an odd-looking pen. He had paused in what he was doing to address Cy.

Cy gulped. An answer seemed to be expected of him. 'Indeed,' he said. 'Indeed.'

The boy laughed. 'You are funny. I'm glad that my father bought you to be my personal slave.'

Cy's heart crashed. 'Slave?' he said. 'I am your slave?'

The boy nodded. 'Surely you remember? My father bought you yesterday. In the market at the port of Ostia when he was on his way to Rome. I think you had just arrived with other captives from Britain.'

Cy shook his head. Would he never be able to organize his dreams the way he wanted to? If he was going to visit ancient Rome he would much rather be a commander in the Roman army or a Master of Gladiators. He was seriously fed up with this. In his Viking dream he had been a swineherd and now in ancient Rome he was a slave. 'So, I am a slave,' he said sadly.

'Don't look so upset,' said the boy. 'Being a Roman slave has many advantages. You will have special privileges, and may even one day be a free man. My father said that you seemed well educated so you have also to be my tutor. Tell me what you think of my drawing.' He held out his piece of paper. 'I am making a drawing of a dog. It is a copy of one of my father's mosaics. It is a savage dog. Underneath it I will write, "Beware of the dog".'

Cy looked at the boy's drawing. A fierce-looking dog with pointed ears snarled up at him. 'It's good,' he said. 'What is your name?'

'Linus.'

'Linus,' said Cy, 'it might make it more lifelike if you did not show it at rest. You could show the dog about to pounce, for instance. Action can make the picture more interesting.'

'Thank you,' said Linus happily. 'I draw many sketches. I want to be as my father and make designs for mosaics. I'd like to do scenes of the city and the countryside, but it is a picture of a dog that householders want on the ground at the entrance to their homes.'

Linus's mother had heard them talking. She glanced over. 'We should buy some cloth to make the new slave some suitable clothes.'

Cy looked in alarm at the short tunic that the boy beside him was wearing. 'I am *not* wearing a skirt,' he said.

Linus's mother frowned. 'A slave does not dictate what he will or will not wear.'

'He should not,' Linus agreed with his mother. 'But Father said he was mine. And I say that he should be allowed to wear the clothes of his own country.' He looked at Cy's sweatshirt and trousers. 'Strange as they may be.'

'Very well,' said his mother. 'We will take this piece of purple cloth. I do not have time to argue with my daughter. I leave tonight to join my husband in Rome, and must ensure that she has adequate clothes before I go.'

Behind the older woman's back Cy saw the shopkeeper Darius and Linus's sister Rhea Silvia exchange glances.

Then the scene in front of his eyes shuddered and settled.

'What was that?' asked Cy.

'It is August,' said Rhea Silvia's mother. 'The earth always trembles in the hot summer months.'

Cy screwed up his eyes. The figures in front of him were again moving in a strange slipping movement.

'Let us go.'

It was his mother's voice that he heard now.

'Stop dreaming, Cy.'

Cy blinked his eyes wide open. His mum was waving her hands in front of his face. She bent to take a closer look at him. 'You've gone very pale, you look as though you need some fresh air. Come on. I'm giving up on this shopping trip. I'll drop you at the library on the way home.'

CHAPTER V

'All the books on volcanoes are out,' said the librarian, 'and the Internet terminals are booked up for the rest of the day.'

'No way!' said Cy. 'I need information and our computer at home is being repaired.'

'The best I can do is book you an Internet session for tomorrow.' She flicked open the computer appointment book. 'It is Cyrus Peters, isn't it?' She smiled as Cy nodded. 'I thought I recognized your face, Cy. I'll put you down for Internet access tomorrow afternoon,' she went on. 'Try not to forget, because after tomorrow we'll be closed for the bank holiday weekend, and it might be the last chance you get to finish your homework before school begins.' She gave Cy a slip of paper which showed the appointment time for his Internet booking.

Cy held the piece of paper and thought about where he could put it so that he would not forget about his appointment tomorrow. The trouble was, he forgot lots of things. Most times he didn't even know he'd forgotten them. And often it was really important things, like one night when his mum phoned and asked him to let his dad know that she was waiting to be picked up from working late at her school. Cy had hung up the phone in the hall and walked towards the kitchen with the message clear in his head. Yet the moment he walked through the kitchen door it had gone. Just like that. He was halfway through helping his dad cook dinner when his mum phoned again twenty minutes later and neither she nor dad was best pleased. His dad because he'd had to cook most of the dinner, and his mum because she had been hanging around in the rain. The thing that no-one seemed to understand, not even Cy, was that he didn't even remember things after being reminded about them. He could only take his mum's word for it that she had asked him to ask Dad to come and collect her. Cy could remember speaking to her on the telephone but not exactly what she had said.

Similar things happened to Cy all the time so he knew that it was he who was at fault. At school, or with his friends, or at home, his brain frequently jumped out of gear and sometimes even juddered to a complete halt. Then everybody became exasperated with him. Though actually, thought Cy, it wasn't quite true to say that absolutely *everybody* lost their patience. His grampa and his teacher, Mrs Chalmers, were more understanding. Mrs Chalmers always said that she was sure that Cy was gifted in other ways. And Cy's grampa always said that the best thing to do in life was to get on with what you had, and think up ways of dealing with what you hadn't.

Cy's grampa had been in the War. He'd served with Field Marshal Montgomery in the Western Desert and anytime Monty had come past Grampa's tent for a bit of a chat on how the war was going, Grampa had been able to advise him about planning ahead, as he told Cy: *'Forward thinking, that's what I said to Monty. Forward thinking helps overcome the odds.'* Grampa called it his 'Strategy to Survive'.

And he had devised a strategy for Cy to remember things. Cy felt in the pocket of his jeans for the big brass curtain ring Grampa had given him. Using the curtain ring was Grampa's idea so that Cy would know there was something he had to remember. Cy wrapped the piece of paper with his appointment time around the curtain ring. He was sure that he wouldn't forget to look at it tonight and tomorrow. Well . . . he was *almost* sure.

The librarian gave Cy a searching glance. 'As this is the umpteenth enquiry on volcanoes that I've had today I'm guessing there's a school project due to be handed in quite soon. Would I be correct?'

'Tuesday,' said Cy, 'when school goes back after the break. We have to hand in a fully documented project on volcanoes.'

'Well, you had better get started then.' The librarian raised her head and looked across the library. 'There's a boy and a girl working with some reference books at the table by the window. They'll probably let you share.'

Cy looked over to where the librarian was pointing. He sucked in his breath. Eddie and Chloe! The Mean Machines! They were the two nastiest people in the whole school, and they always

45

seemed to pick on him especially. They were the last people he wanted to see.

'I'll leave it until later—' Cy began.

'Later will be too late,' said the librarian. 'Remember, the library will be closed for the long weekend. You can't put it off any longer, Cy.' She had come round to Cy's side of the counter and was now steering him towards the table in the corner.

'Let Cy share these books with you,' she said to Eddie and Chloe. 'He is researching the same subject.' She smiled at all three of them. 'If you are doing the same project then you probably know each other anyway.'

Eddie nudged Chloe. 'It's Cy,' he said in a treacly sweet voice.

Chloe gave the librarian one of her special friendly smiles that she reserved for adults in authority. 'Of course we can share. That's no problem.' She moved swiftly to the next chair, making a space between her and Eddie.

'Look,' said Eddie. 'Here's a space right here for Cy.'

The librarian pulled the chair out, and before he could help himself Cy stumbled forwards and sat down, trapped between his tormentors.

'Good to see you, Cy,' said Chloe in a sing-song voice. 'Come and join us, Cy.' She waited until the librarian had returned to the counter. 'Sewer-Cy,' she said.

Eddie leaned closer so that he was crushing Cy's arm and elbow. 'Why do you bother doing projects?' he sneered. 'Your writing is so awful that nobody will be able to read it.'

'That's right,' Chloe chimed in. 'If we're preparing things for display in class Mrs Chalmers always gives you drawing to do 'cos your writing is so scrawly.'

Cy felt one of his panic attacks beginning. He desperately began one of Grampa's stress-suppressers: counting to ten very slowly and thinking of the shapes of the numbers while doing it. But it was no use. He couldn't get beyond number 3. The shape would not form in his head. It was ridiculous! He was much too old for this to be happening to him. For goodness' sake! He *must* be able to count to 3! Cy began again: 1 was a wizard wand; 2, an elegant swan serene on a flat lake; 3 . . . where was 3? He knew that he always thought of it as a crabby-looking little number, unfinished and gaping with an open mouth that seemed to be saying rude things . . . a bit like Chloe . . .

'Look.' Chloe shoved her finger right into Cy's face. 'Look, Eddie, Cy's gone into one of his day-dreams.'

'Whaaa?' said Cy, coming back to where he was. He looked at Chloe's face. Her mouth *did* look like the number 3. Aha! He had it now in his head. Number 3 – with its wide mouth and chin jutting out at the bottom. And it had worked! Grampa's stress-suppresser had actually worked! Cy had stopped listening to the Mean Machines and now he felt a lot calmer. 'I'm going to have a look at these books,' he said quietly. 'I'll take them one at a time to the next table and bring them back to you when I've done.' He began to get up out of his chair.

Eddie looped his foot under Cy's chair leg and dragged it forwards. Cy fell back down again.

'Don't be silly,' said Cy. 'Let me go or I'll call the librarian over.'

'Tell-tale,' said Eddie.

'Clype,' said Chloe.

'No,' said Cy. He quoted from the 'IS' and 'IS NOT' anti-bullying posters that their headteacher had put up in the corridors and cloakrooms in school. '"Reporting bullying IS NOT telling tales. Reporting bullying IS responsible citizenship." So –' he looked from Chloe to Eddie – 'let me go or I'll yell.'

Eddie moved his face so close that his breath was hot against Cy's face. 'You won't yell and you won't tell, because that only makes it worse, doesn't it?' He kicked Cy's chair. 'Doesn't it?'

'The librarian will hear you,' Cy said desperately.

Chloe looked quickly towards the library desk. The librarian was working at the computer terminal, but was still within sight and hearing. 'All right,' said Chloe, 'you can share with us. But I'm using all of these books at the moment.' She grabbed four of the reference books.

'And I'm using these two,' said Eddie, putting his hand on the rest.

'Oh look,' said Chloe in a sweet voice. 'There's this ickle little book here.' She picked up a very old small booklet and slid it along the table to Cy. 'That's about your level anyway.'

Cy looked at the cover of the book. It showed a scene from ancient Roman times with a volcano erupting in the background. But it wasn't the volcanic eruption that caught Cy's attention. It was the details in the foreground that made him look closer. There was something vaguely familiar about the crowded market place. Shop fronts and

stalls were piled high with goods of all kinds –
fruit and wine in large jars, double-handled
amphorae, fish on marble slabs, cooking pots and
reddish-brown dishes of Samian ware from Gaul.
In the foreground was a cloth merchant, with bolts
of silk and leather skins, bales of cotton and
embroidered cushions. And there was the cloth
merchant himself. An older man, not clean-shaven
as was the Roman custom, but with a small
pointed beard.

Cy gasped and looked again.

It was the cloth merchant from his dream. The
one who had been trying so hard to sell the length
of cloth to Rhea Silvia!

CHAPTER VI

'D arius!' cried Cy.

'What?' said Chloe and Eddie together.

'The Roman merchant –' Cy pointed excitedly at the front of the little booklet – 'his name is Darius.'

'How can you ever know that?' demanded Eddie. 'You've only just looked at the book. You can't know the name of the person on the cover.'

'But I do,' Cy babbled on without thinking. 'I met him – well, not *met* him exactly, but I heard him talking.'

'Where?' demanded Chloe. 'Where would you possibly hear this, this . . .' she flipped the book towards her, '. . . this . . . shopkeeper actually talking?'

'It was when I was dreaming,' said Cy. 'I'd travelled to—'

'Give us a break,' said Eddie. 'I do *not* want to hear about any of your idiotic dreams.'

'But we *should* listen,' said Chloe sarcastically. 'This is Cy's wonderful imagination that Mrs Chalmers always goes on about. Everyone says that Cy is so clever at making up stories.' Chloe stuck her tongue out. 'You are such a Super-Cy, aren't you?'

Cy's face went red.

'No he's not,' said Eddie. 'He must have seen this book earlier. I'll bet it tells you all of that somewhere inside.'

'Of course,' said Chloe. She turned to Cy. 'You came to the library earlier in the holidays and you've already done some work on the project, haven't you?'

'No,' said Cy, 'I haven't. It's just that sometimes when I dream I can choose . . .' He hesitated and then stopped. He'd love to tell Eddie and Chloe all about how his dreams sometimes flipped over.

And rather than being inside his head the way most people's were, occasionally it went the other way and he was actually inside the dream. If only he could boast about meeting his Dream Master and knowing partly how to use the dreamcloak, which meant that occasionally he could dream up his own dreams the way he wanted them to be. (Except that it didn't always work out as he planned.) Cy looked at Eddie and Chloe. They'd never believe him, and anyway he didn't know if he wanted to share such a terrific secret with the Mean Machines. He hadn't even told his friends Vicky, or Innis, or Basra.

Eddie leaned across the table and took the book from Chloe's hands. 'Let's have a look inside. It probably gives you the shopkeeper's name on the very first page.'

Chloe snatched at the book. 'I had it first,' she said.

'Well, I've got it now,' said Eddie, pulling it back.

There was a ripping sound as the book cover tore.

Eddie flung the book in front of Cy. 'It was him,' he said at once, 'wasn't it, Chloe?'

Cy felt himself grow hot and cold all at once. The librarian had appeared and was gazing severely at all three of them.

'It is really fortunate for all of you that that book-let is locally produced and there is plenty of old stock available. But I am still not happy with your behaviour.'

'We aren't to blame,' said Chloe. 'Everything was fine until Cy arrived. It's all *his* fault.'

'I don't think so, young lady,' said the librarian. 'I know Cy. He comes in quite often. Whereas you two have been sitting here most of the day not doing very much. I'd like the three of you to sit at separate tables. That way you might all get a bit more work done.' She examined the book in her hand. 'You're lucky that this is not valuable and can be repaired. Please sort yourselves out by the time I return with it.'

Eddie and Chloe got up as the librarian took the booklet away to mend the page with some clear tape.

'I'm going home now anyway,' said Eddie. 'You coming?' he asked Chloe.

Chloe nodded and angrily began to pack up her things. She glared at Cy and hissed, 'No-one gets me into trouble and gets away with it.'

'Don't you ever think that it is you who gets yourself into trouble?' replied Cy bravely.

'The next time we meet it won't be *me* getting

told off,' said Chloe grimly as she and Eddie walked towards the exit.

At the library entrance Eddie paused and pulled at Chloe's sleeve. 'Look,' he whispered. He pointed to the computer appointment book which was lying open on top of the librarian's desk. 'Cy's got a booking for the Internet tomorrow.'

Chloe leaned over and studied the page. 'What time is he coming to the library tomorrow?' Her finger found the place on the page. 'Right.' Her eyes glittered and her face twisted in a sour smile. 'I think we can arrange it that tomorrow Mr Cyrus Peters will get a very nasty surprise.'

Cy waited until the librarian brought back the mended booklet and then he studied the front cover as she tidied away the other books which Chloe and Eddie had been using. Cy could see more of the street scene than he had seen in his dream. In his dream he had been almost inside the shop, but this view was from the street itself and showed the stalls and shops in greater detail. Next to the cloth merchant's was a cobbler's stall where the cobbler sat on his stool working at his last. He was surrounded by foot templates, and pieces of leather cut to shape to cover soles and heels. Behind him were shelf alcoves where pairs of sandals and shoes were stored. Further along was a perfume stall with pots of alabaster and marble filled with creams and oils. Rows of glass bottles and phials of many colours containing scented essences sparkled on wooden racks. A lady with elaborately coiled hair was sampling one of the perfumes. She held the lid in the shape of a pea-cock tail in one hand while she sniffed the contents of the bottle. Beside that was a fishmonger's shop with the biggest variety of fish Cy had ever seen.

Cy traced the shapes and colours with his fin-gers. The text on the back cover told him that this had been an affluent town with goods coming from all over the Roman Empire and beyond. Silks and spices from China, perfume and ivory from India, grain from Egypt and fish brought in by the many boats that fished the sea close to the town. The stalls along the main shopping street, called in this book the Via dell'Abbondanza, were always busy. Had all this been going on outside the shop while he sat inside discussing mosaic-making with Linus?

'What I don't understand,' Cy said, 'is, if this is a book about volcanoes, why do we have a scene showing ancient Rome?'

'It isn't Rome,' said the librarian. 'It *is* Roman

times, but this is not a scene from ancient Rome. It is the market place of a town quite close to Rome where there was a famous volcanic eruption. Almost without warning the nearby mountain, Vesuvius, threw out boiling ash and mud for days. The population was wiped out.'

'When was this?' Cy asked. 'Where was the town?'

'It happened in AD seventy-nine,' said the librarian, 'near Naples. The town was called Pompeii.'

'Pompeii,' repeated Cy.

'Yes.' The librarian looked at the book again. 'We have more copies of this book, so I'll let you borrow this one if you like.'

Cy opened the book carefully. There was another scene inside the front cover. It depicted the inside of one of the shops. The cloth merchant's shop. Cy's eyes began to blur as he gazed at the interior. There was a woman sitting on a long bench. Directly in front of her was a young girl who had draped a length of fabric about herself. The older woman's head was to one side as she studied her daughter critically. A slave held a mirror so that the young girl could see herself. The material draped in long folds to the ground and was a beautiful reddish purple, a deep Tyrian-purple cloth.

Cy's hand shook as he laid the book out flat before him on the library table. The two torn halves didn't match together exactly. And so it was that the boy sitting to one side looked as though he had turned his head to look away from the scene; his gaze travelled outside the shop, beyond the streets and time of ancient Pompeii to . . .

Cy's heart did a half-beat out of time. The boy had moved. His mouth was open slightly, as though he was speaking.

'Help!' he seemed to cry out to Cy. 'Help us!'

CHAPTER VII

Cy walked slowly home from the library with the book about Pompeii in his rucksack. His mind was struggling to keep up with everything that had happened to him today. He'd got up – he could remember that quite clearly. Then he remembered deciding, as there were only a few days left before school began, that it might be a good idea to do some work on his project on volcanoes.

Cy frowned in concentration as he tried to recall the next part of his day. His Dream Master had

appeared . . . That was it! His Dream Master had been moaning on about his dreamcloak becoming worn out because Cy dreamed such vivid dreams, and then, and then . . . Cy's thoughts and his pace began to quicken as the morning's events came back to him. He had pulled out his own little piece of dreamsilk from below his chest of drawers, and by some strange happening it had become larger and more powerful than it had been previously! Then somehow both he and the Dream Master had been whisked to volcano after volcano in TimeSpace, until finally they were in vineyards outside a town, which Cy now knew to be Pompeii. He had hardly got into that dream when his mum had woken him up and dragged him off to the shops with Lauren, whereupon Cy had ended up in a shop in Pompeii . . . and now he was back here.

Cy hated dreams like that, all disjointed with bits that he couldn't remember properly. He went over it again in his head. He and the Dream Master had travelled to some different volcanoes, eventually they had gone together to the vineyards, then . . .

Cy stopped still in the street. His heart and his head lurched together. Where *was* the Dream

Master? He hadn't been with Cy in the shop in Pompeii . . . and . . . he hadn't returned with him to twenty-first-century Britain, that was for sure. So where was he? And – cold fear swept over Cy – wherever he was, he was stuck there. Because it hadn't been the dreamcloak that had taken them through TimeSpace, it had been the little scrap of dreamsilk. And Cy still had that little scrap in his pocket.

His Dream Master was separated from his dreamcloak! The dreamcloak that Cy had left lying on top of his bed for anyone to find! And Lauren and his mum would have returned to the house ages ago! Cy began to run.

He crashed through the kitchen door. His mum was sitting staring at a mug of tea. She had on her I've-been-shopping-with-Lauren face and gave Cy a brief smile as he raced past her.

'Did you get the information you needed at the library?' she called after him as he took the stairs two at a time.

'Going back tomorrow,' Cy shouted. He flung open his bedroom door and felt a flood of relief. Everything was where he had left it. The dream-cloak was a mass of pale grey on his bed.

The room was clammy with the heat of the

afternoon. Cy threw his rucksack on the bed and took out the library book about Pompeii. At that moment his bedroom door opened and Lauren came in. She had on the short cotton shift dress that she had worn to go shopping, but had draped her new school tie around her neck.

'Knock before entering,' said Cy.

'Don't be so rude,' said his sister. 'I only came to offer you some help, Sproglet.'

'Help?' said Cy suspiciously. It wasn't normal for Lauren to be friendly to him. Although the fact that she had called him 'Sproglet' was a good sign. Usually the names his sister used when speaking to him were much worse, ranging from 'Tiny Toad' to 'Cyber Stew', with a few particularly nasty ones that she reserved for special occasions.

'Yes, help. I guess I owe you a favour for throwing a wobbly earlier today so that Mum felt she had to cut short the ghastly shopping trip.'

'Oh . . . right.' Cy decided not to tell Lauren that, in his opinion, the main reason that Mum had given up on the shopping was Lauren's own awful behaviour. 'I don't need any help right now,' he said, moving forward to block her way.

Lauren side-stepped Cy and walked further into

his room. 'I thought you were researching some project or other?'

Cy could feel himself losing control of the situation. Lauren being kind was marginally worse than Lauren being a pest. When she was horrible to him at least he knew what to expect. Lauren in helpful mode was unpredictable.

'No, everything's fine,' said Cy, and smiled a great big smile to show how fine everything was.

'Well, now I know it's not,' said Lauren. 'Otherwise you wouldn't be grinning like the Cheshire Cat. You probably have to hand in your project when school begins. Our computer is being repaired and your writing is none too good, so I could help you with some stuff if you like.'

'No. Thanks. But no, thanks. Really. Thanks. But no.' Cy was aware he was gibbering.

A mad panic seized him as he watched Lauren wander about his room touching things. She caught sight of the little book on Pompeii still resting on his bed.

'If you're doing Pompeii,' she said, 'I've got some stuff in an old box file that might be helpful. I did that as a project when I was your age.'

'Nope,' Cy yelped. ''s OK.'

Before Cy could stop her Lauren flopped down

on his bed. 'It's so hot,' she said.

Cy gaped at her in absolute terror. She was lying right beside the dreamcloak! His fingers felt for his own scrap of dreamsilk in his pocket. He had his school project to do *and* a lost Dream Master; the last thing he needed was his sister somehow getting into his Pompeii dream and messing it up. I could push her off the bed onto the floor, Cy thought. He reached out his hand and touched his sister on the arm. The instant he did so, he knew that he had made a mistake.

'Omigosh! Omigollygosh!'

The thought about Pompeii was in his head and he couldn't get it out fast enough. The dreamsilk scorched his hand. There was a blazing spark and a tremendous fizzle of noise, and Lauren and he went tumbling through Time.

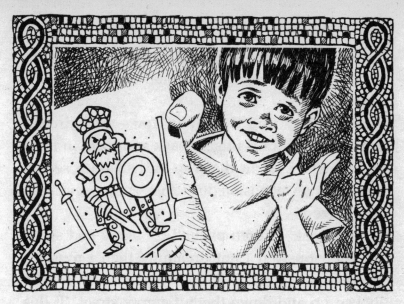

CHAPTER VIII

Cy recovered first. The fact that he knew roughly where they would land helped. He snatched the book from Lauren's hand and stuffed it and the piece of dreamsilk into his pocket as he looked around him. They were outside in a cobbled street, but it was not the Via dell'Abbondanza with its busy shops, where he had been before. This was a quiet residential tree-lined avenue. Thank goodness, thought Cy, no-one has seen us. If I can think fast enough I can get us back to my bedroom before Lauren realizes what has happened.

'What's going on?' said Lauren, sitting up slowly. 'Was that an explosion? Where is this place?'

'Dreaming,' said Cy firmly. 'You – are – dreaming.' He waved his fingers back and forth in front of Lauren's eyes in the way he had once seen a hypnotist on television do. 'Close – your – eyes. Go – to – sleep.'

'Stop that.' Lauren pushed Cy away and stood up. 'Obviously if I am dreaming then I must be sleeping and I can't fall asleep again, can I?' She looked up and down the hot empty street. 'If this is a dream then it's pretty boring, and it's even hotter here than in the real world, so I think I'll just wake up, thanks very much.'

'Fine,' said Cy. 'Great. Super.' He reached for his piece of dreamsilk. 'Just give me two seconds,' he muttered, 'to gather my mind together and focus us back where we came from.'

'Who is this?' said a voice behind Cy.

Cy turned and saw Rhea Silvia standing in the doorway of a nearby house. 'My sister,' he gulped.

'Ahh, your sister,' said Rhea Silvia softly. 'That is where you have been. How kind you are. I will explain to my mother that you ran off to find your sister. It is very thoughtful of you to do this.'

'Thoughtful!' said Lauren. 'That's the first time I've ever heard anyone call Cy thoughtful.'

'Why, yes, I think he is,' said Rhea Silvia. 'I would wish that my brother Linus would look out for me if we were captured by our enemies. I will ask if I can have a personal slave. After all, Linus has one, so I don't see why I shouldn't have one also. Come –' she beckoned with her hand – 'let us sit by the fountain. You can help me sort out the purchases I made while shopping.'

'A slave!' cried Lauren as they followed Rhea Silvia into the central courtyard of the house. 'Am I a slave?'

Cy closed his eyes. Now there really *would* be an explosion. He couldn't imagine Lauren taking kindly to being a slave.

'Yes,' said Rhea Silvia. 'You and your brother must be house slaves until you can earn your freedom.'

Lauren spoke to Cy in a whisper. 'What *interesting* dreams you have, Cy. I had no idea.'

Cy's mouth gaped open. 'You don't mind being a Roman slave?'

'I think I might like it,' said Lauren. 'As long as it isn't a galley slave. I know *nothing* about cooking.'

'Eh?'

Lauren hit her forehead with the palm of her hand. 'Duh. Joke, Cy.' She glanced round her. 'This looks like a very up-market household. What are my duties?' she asked Rhea Silvia.

'If my father will buy you, then you might dress my hair and help me with my make-up,' said Rhea Silvia.

'Way to go!' said Lauren. 'That's for me.' She stepped forward and peered closely at Rhea Silvia. 'Your eye make-up is *fantastic*. How do you get that line to extend across your eyelid without smudging in this heat?'

'Kohl,' said Rhea Silvia, 'from Egypt. I mix it with a little soap and then use a fine brush. But the brush must be of genuine camel hair.'

She in her turn was studying Lauren's clothes. 'Your clothes are . . . unusual,' she said. 'May I try this?' She pointed to the school tie draped around Lauren's neck.

'You can keep it as far as I'm concerned,' said Lauren. She handed her striped tie over, and then, seeing that Rhea Silvia had no idea how to make the knot, she did it for her.

Rhea Silvia leaned over and looked at her reflection in the water of the fountain. 'None of my friends will have anything like this. I cannot imagine how anyone thought to team these colours together.'

'Believe me, neither can I,' said Lauren. 'But *your* clothes are gorgeous. That is the most fabby colour I've ever seen.' She fingered the cloth of Rhea Silvia's new skirt.

Rhea Silvia looked pleased. 'The material is from a town in the Lebanon called Tyre. It is the only place that you can get such a shade. They have the secret of the purple dye. Here –' she offered the skirt length to Lauren – 'let us go inside to my room and see how it looks on you.'

'I thought you liked short skirts,' said Cy as Lauren wrapped the floor-length piece of material around herself.

'When in Rome,' said Lauren.

'Pardon?'

'It's an expression,' said Lauren. And, as Cy still looked bewildered, added, 'It's a thing people say, "When in Rome, do as the Romans do." It means adopt the style and customs of the people that you are with at the moment,' said Lauren, and she flounced after Rhea.

Cy didn't like to point out that they weren't in Rome, exactly. They were actually in Pompeii. Best not to, though, he thought as he trotted after the two girls; it might panic his sister and he felt that he could panic enough for both of them. Also he didn't intend to stay here for very much longer. He would have to stop Lauren getting too friendly with Rhea Silvia and try to have a moment alone with his sister. Then hopefully he'd be able to use the dreamsilk and get Lauren back to his room quickly enough for her to believe that this was a dream.

Cy spoke politely to Rhea Silvia. 'My sister cannot become your slave. She belongs to a household far beyond the town, and has only been allowed out for a few hours to deliver a message.'

'No way!' Lauren hissed. 'I want to stay here.'

'It's my dream,' said Cy in a low voice. 'What I say goes.'

Lauren made a rude face at her brother and appealed to Rhea Silvia. 'I'd like to be *your* slave.'

'When my father returns from Rome, I will ask him to buy you from your present owner,' said Rhea Silvia. 'Meanwhile perhaps you would tell me how it is that you braid your hair in that manner?'

'Sure,' said Lauren. 'Want me to do yours like it?'

'Cyrus!'

Cy turned his head and saw that Rhea Silvia's brother Linus had arrived by the fountain. Cy paused. He would have to let his sister go into the interior of the house. As a slave he could not ignore Linus's call. He ran back hurriedly to the courtyard.

'You must look at my new drawing.' The boy thrust his sketch under Cy's nose. 'I took your advice and made it more active. It is one of the gladiators.'

'Terrific,' said Cy, hardly glancing at Linus's parchment.

'He is a new fighter,' said Linus. 'Such trouble he is causing. He claims he is a great lord but he has no lineage or family to speak up for him. He was captured thieving from a house on the mountain slopes outside Herculaneum. Tell me what you think. Have I captured his posture?'

'It's good,' said Cy, his mind still on Lauren. How long could two girls spend talking about make-up? A very long time, if the length of the sessions in the bathroom at home when Lauren's friends Baz and Cartwheel visited were anything to go by. Cy glanced again briefly at Linus's drawing. 'It's very—' He stopped and looked again.

'Omigosh! Omigollygosh!' Cy pointed a shaking finger at Linus's drawing of a gladiator in full combat gear. It showed a small angry kilted figure partly encased in body armour, with leather greaves to protect his legs; holding a shield and wielding a short sword. From underneath the helmet glared the face of the Dream Master.

'Where did you see this man?' Cy stuttered.

'At the barracks behind the Temple of Isis,' said Linus. 'He is a new gladiator. They call him Dominus Somniorum. He fights on the holiday in two days' time.'

'Fights? In two days?' Cy's voice came out in a strangulated yelp.

'Yes,' said Linus. 'In the Amphitheatre. He fights to the death.'

CHAPTER IX

'To the death!'

'Surely you must know this.' Linus looked into Cy's stricken face. 'Even far away in Britain you must have heard of the great gladiator fights of the mighty Roman Empire.'

'Yes . . . but . . .' Cy stammered. 'I think I might know this man. Is there any way that I could speak to him?'

'I could take you to the Barracks of the Gladiators,' said Linus. 'My friends and I know a way in where we watch the gladiators practising in the courtyard.

If we go now we might catch sight of this new fighter.'

Cy hesitated. Could he safely leave Lauren while he went with Linus to visit the Dream Master? He looked at his piece of dreamsilk. It was turning pale. 'A dream has its own time,' the Dream Master had told him. If he waited much longer he and Lauren could be stuck in ancient times for ever. The Dream Master was right. It *did* require mental gymnastics and concentration to be a Dream Master. Cy felt totally inadequate.

'You want to see him, don't you?' Linus had been watching the expression on Cy's face.

Cy nodded. 'Yes, but I don't know if I have enough time. I've ... I've ... got to get my sister back home ... er, to the house – household where she should be.'

Linus placed his hand on Cy's arm. 'It is August and very hot. Everyone sleeps for an hour or so after the midday meal. My mother has gone to visit my father at his mosaic workshop in Rome. My sister and yours will talk and then eat and then rest. We will have time if we run quickly. You could see the new gladiator and be back before they wake up. I will show you the way.'

Cy decided to take the risk. He needed to see the

Dream Master. He owed it to him to at least let him know where he was. Also . . . he needed advice.

As Linus had predicted, the streets which the two boys ran along were almost deserted. The few people that they met paid no attention to a young boy accompanied by his slave.

'This way,' said Linus. 'At the crossroads we take the street towards the Odeon. At the next block, near the Temple of Isis, is an opening. It has not yet been repaired since the earth quaked and destroyed the buildings the year that my sister was born. If we take that passageway it will bring us out at the barracks.'

Cy followed Linus between the buildings until they came to a double-storeyed block set round a large grassed arena.

'Here,' Linus whispered. He pulled Cy behind a pillar. 'The instructors know that boys come to watch the mock fights. They do not mind as long as we are not too noisy.'

Cy looked around. There were wooden posts embedded in the grass and men were hacking and chopping at these with their swords. Other men were grappling with each other, or fighting in pairs, or practising spear throws.

'I don't see him,' Cy whispered.

'If he is being difficult he may be confined to his cubicle.' Linus pointed at the building. 'The instructors are on the upper floor. The gladiators occupy the small cubicles underneath.'

'Once they are outside, why don't these gladiators run away?' Cy nodded at the men who were on the grass.

'It is a great honour to be a gladiator,' said Linus. 'Many men volunteer to fight.'

Cy and Linus began to walk round under the covered walkway. It didn't take them very long to find the locked cell which contained the Dream Master. The little man leaped to his feet immediately. He pushed his face through the bars.

'Where is my cloak?' he demanded.

'You cannot fight with a cloak if you have a sword and shield,' said Linus. 'You are to be one of the *bestiarii* and they do not carry cloaks.'

'I need my cloak,' the Dream Master hissed at Cy. 'You've been back to your own time, I can tell, so where is it?'

'I didn't bring it,' said Cy. 'Things got . . . complicated.'

'Complicated, shmonkplicated,' snapped the Dream Master. 'We'll just have to use your piece of dreamsilk then. Come over here beside me and focus your mind so that I can escape.'

'I can't use it to take you back to your dream-cloak,' said Cy miserably. 'I think there is only enough energy in it to take me and one other back through TimeSpace to the twenty-first century.'

'And what's the problem?' snarled the Dream Master. 'Which A. N. Other apart from myself would you be taking back?'

'Lauren,' said Cy.

'Lauren!' screeched the Dream Master. 'Your *sister* Lauren?'

Cy nodded.

'How in the name of Volatile Vulcan did your sister Lauren end up in ancient Pompeii?'

'I suppose it was my fault really,' said Cy. 'Your dreamcloak was lying on my bed and she sat down beside it. I was so busy making sure that she didn't go near the dreamcloak that I forgot I was holding my piece of dreamsilk and then I touched her arm. I was trying not to think about Pompeii. But sometimes when you try not to think about something, that's the very thing you just can't stop thinking about. It just sort of . . . happened.'

'Sort of . . . happened,' the Dream Master mimicked Cy nastily. 'How many times have I told you, you . . . you . . . Dimwitted Doughnut, that when you are master of a dream things don't just "happen". You guide the events, you look after the Story. You . . . you . . .' The Dream Master slumped against the wall. 'You really have got to get a grip.'

There was a silence. Linus looked at the Dream Master. 'I know now why they say that you have a mighty temper. You will fight well.'

'I have no intention of fighting anyone, any-where, anytime!' roared the Dream Master. 'I will not fight any man. If they drag me into an arena I will sit down in the sand. I WILL NOT FIGHT!'

Linus leaped back from the door of the cell. 'We must go now,' he said to Cy.

'But you do see that before I do anything else I need to take Lauren back first?' Cy begged the Dream Master as he turned to follow Linus. 'I'm not deserting you. I mean, just think what it would be like if Lauren realized what was going on. She'd want to use the dreamcloak too.'

The Dream Master shuddered. Eventually he nodded. 'All right. Go and return Lauren to her own time.'

'After I do that I'll come back for you straight away,' said Cy. He began to walk away.

The Dream Master reached out through the bars and grasped Cy's arm with a strong grip. 'Listen to me. You will be travelling through TimeSpace without me. Because I do not have my dreamcloak I will not be able to come to your aid if things go wrong. You are very inexperienced so you must take care. Be watchful. Consider what you do, say, or think. You are on your own, Cy.'

Cy ran quickly to the corner of the barracks where Linus was waiting. 'Where does the actual combat take place?' he asked him.

'In the Amphitheatre at the other end of the town. There is more room there, seating for twenty thousand people and space for the animals.'

'Animals?' Cy repeated. 'Like cats and dogs?'

Linus shook his head. 'More fierce than that. It is mainly wild animals, from Africa and India. There is even an elephant which leads the procession of combatants into the arena.'

'Do these animals perform?' A slow cold dread began to stalk through Cy's mind.

Linus gave Cy a puzzled look. 'Perform?'

'What do they do?' asked Cy. 'Why do they have these animals at the Amphitheatre?'

'Why, for the gladiators to fight,' said Linus. 'I told you earlier; it has been decided that the little man should be one of the *bestiarii*. Look.' He pointed to a poster which was attached to the wall

of the barracks. 'It tells what the holiday pro-
gramme will be. See there, the first fight of the
morning is your friend Dominus Somniorum.
They must believe him when he shouts that he will
not fight with any man. So they have not placed
him in combat with another gladiator. He is
matched against a lion.'

CHAPTER X

When they got back to the villa Cy lay down and waited until Linus fell asleep. The household was quiet as he walked softly along the passage to Rhea Silvia's room and drew back the curtain. Lauren was on a little pallet at the entrance. Her breathing was steady and her eyes closed. Cy kneeled beside her and lightly took her hand. With the fingers of his other hand he touched the dreamsilk in his pocket and carefully, carefully, remembering all the Dream Master's instructions, he lifted them both back to his bedroom in the twenty-first century.

Cy crept past his sleeping sister. He glided out of his bedroom onto the hall landing. Silently he opened the door of the laundry cupboard and grabbed an old beach towel from the bottom of the pile. Then he tiptoed back into his room and spread it out on the floor beside his bed. Gently lifting the edge of his duvet furthest away from Lauren, he tipped it up so that the Dreamcloak ruffled sideways and fell onto the towel. Was it true what the Dream Master had said? That the cloak was becoming worn out by Cy's adventures? It certainly looked floppy and lifeless.

Cy had no idea what to do about it. Did it need its own true owner to energize it? And why had the Dream Master expressly forbidden him to try to reconnect the torn piece? Surely it would meld together in some way, as electricity could run into a battery and recharge it?

Cy thought for a moment about what the Dream Master had said when he had suggested this. 'Yes, if you put the two pieces together they might connect. Like a stray atom in a nuclear fission. Think of the sun exploding and you might have some inkling of the outcome.'

Cy remembered the expression on the little

82

man's face as he had studied the torn piece when he first noticed that it had changed. The Dream Master had looked afraid, afraid and unsure . . .

Cy examined the remnant of dreamcloak that now belonged to him. It *had* changed and – Cy's eyes narrowed – since his adventure with Lauren, it had changed again. It was bigger and more . . . Cy searched for the right word to describe it . . . more . . . complete. That was it! The edges were less ragged. The energy that it contained seemed to flow out to the perimeter and then back to the centre. But where was the centre?

Cy felt his skin begin to tingle, a soft itch starting just below the surface of his body. It was coming from inside him, somewhere within his mind, yet he knew that it had been triggered by something outside. The dreamsilk! He felt himself being drawn to do something, to go somewhere, but he was not able to know exactly what it was.

Cy pulled his mind back to the present situation. He tucked his piece of dreamsilk into his pocket and looked around his room. He must find a place to keep his Dream Master's dreamcloak and then get Lauren out of his room. He would have to wait until night-time before he could go back to Pompeii and rescue the Dream Master. Cy glanced out of his window to where the hot August sun was beginning to sink lower in the sky. The gladiator games were only two days away. He didn't have a huge amount of time.

Cy took the four corners of the towel and knotted them together. Where could he hide the dreamcloak so that no-one would find it? It had to be safe from Lauren's prying expeditions and his parents' cleaning excursions. His secret place under his chest of drawers was too small. Cy knelt down and dragged out from underneath his bed the boxes that contained his winter clothes. He opened the lid of one and dumped the bundle on top of some heavy sweaters. Then he shoved the boxes back under his bed. For the moment at least the dreamcloak was safe until he could find a way of reuniting it with its owner.

Lauren was still sleeping. Cy decided not to risk wakening her. He would go downstairs and let her wake up naturally. If she said anything about a dream of ancient Rome he would just laugh.

It worked out simpler than he had imagined. As soon as he appeared downstairs his mum asked him to help her unpack the shopping while she began to prepare dinner. Ten minutes later, when

Lauren appeared sleepily in the doorway, before she had a chance to say anything Cy's mum spoke first.

'You've obviously been having a nap, while Cy and I have been working here. We'll make dinner and you can help Dad clear up the kitchen afterwards.'

Cy avoided meeting Lauren's eyes.

His sister yawned and staggered to the fridge, popped open a can of juice and took a few slurps.

'Did I fall asleep on your bed when we were talking?' she began.

Cy interrupted at once. 'Yeah, and don't ever do it again,' he said. 'Mum, will you tell Lauren to stay out of my room?'

'Lauren,' said Cy's mum in a tone of weary patience, '*please* do not go into your brother's room unless he is agreeable. After all, you don't want him going into your room when you're not there, do you?'

'I was only trying to help him with his project about volcanoes,' said Lauren. She hesitated. 'He was telling me about Pompeii—'

'No,' said Cy quickly. '*You* were telling *me* and then you began to get all mixed up and . . . and . . . fell asleep.'

Cy's mum smiled at both of them in her 'encourage positive behaviour' mode. 'It's good to know that you are supporting each other.'

Lauren grunted. 'Yeah, right.'

Cy could see that his sister was still sleepy and slightly dazed.

'Did you hang up your new school clothes?' Cy's mum asked Lauren.

'Yeah, yeah,' said Lauren.

Cy busied himself setting the table and watched his sister covertly.

Lauren frowned and took a few more sips of her drink. 'I'll leave that box file of mine with the stuff about Pompeii outside your room,' she told Cy. She drifted towards the hall. At the kitchen door she paused and put one hand up to her neck. She turned and, speaking in a low voice so that their mother would not hear her, she asked Cy, 'You wouldn't have seen my new school tie anywhere?'

CHAPTER XI

Later, in his room, Cy took out his notebook and wrote down 'Find Lauren's tie'. He gazed dejectedly at his scribbled writing. No wonder Mrs Chalmers and everyone else complained about it. He could hardly read it himself. He climbed into bed and propped himself up on his pillows. Beside him he placed his own piece of dreamsilk. It was quiet and nearly translucent. There was almost no energy there. That meant he would have to wait for a little while before trying to go back to Pompeii and rescue the Dream

Master. Meanwhile he really should do some work on his school project. Which shouldn't be too difficult now that he had Lauren's notes.

Cy began to brighten up a bit. Volcanoes were very interesting and the eruption at Pompeii seemed particularly exciting. Also, he thought as he opened up the box file that Lauren had given him, the more he knew about Pompeii the easier it would be for him when he returned to help the Dream Master. Cy took out a folder and saw that inside it was a map. He put the folder to one side and opened up the map. It was a plan of the ancient city of Pompeii!

Cy drew in his breath. This would be very useful! He shoved everything else down to the end of his bed and began to study the map. There was a main road, the Via Stabiana, running from one end of the city to the other. Cy followed the line of the road with his finger. And the Via dell'Abbondanza intersected it, making a rightangle fairly near the Barracks of the Gladiators.

'Via dell'Abbondanza.' Cy read the street name out loud. That was where he had first met Rhea Silvia and Linus. In a shop in the Via dell'Abbondanza. What did that street name sound like? 'Bonanza!' It seemed a good name for a street full of shops with goods of every kind from all over the world. Cy scrambled across his bed and got the dictionary from his bookshelf. They were going to study the Romans next term and Mrs Chalmers had told them that lots of words in use in many of today's languages came from Latin. Cy looked up 'Abbondanza' to see if there was anything that looked similar, and saw *abondance*, which was listed as being French for abundance. So Mrs Chalmers was right. It wasn't just English, there were French words that came from Latin. Cy felt a bit like a detective as he tracked the meaning through the dictionary. Eventually he found 'abundant' – and then all its meanings: 'copious supply; great amount'. It *was* a good name for a shopping street, better than naming them after local councillors, Cy thought, as they did today.

Cy looked at the city plan again and began to search for Linus and Rhea Silvia's house. He tried to recall the streets that he'd run along with Linus, how they had passed the Temple of Isis beside the Theatre and the Odeon before coming back onto the main road. He lifted his notebook and began to draw a map, marking with a circle the area where he believed their villa was. Next he looked for the Amphitheatre. It would be a building with a circular shape like the Colosseum in Rome. At last he found it. It was more of an ellipse and was situated at the furthest corner of the town, right at the end of the Via dell'Abbondanza.

'*Porta*,' Cy muttered. Why were so many of these places called '*porta*'? 'Port . . .' It wasn't a port as he knew it, because that would mean it would be situated by the sea, or on water at least. And these couldn't be, as they were all round the city.

'Port . . .' Cy kept his eye on the map and flicked through the pages of his dictionary. 'Port' – he found the word in his dictionary and groaned aloud. There were half a dozen different meanings listed! This was the trouble with language, thought Cy. Just when you thought you had a grasp of it there was always more.

'It's too complicated,' he had complained to Mrs Chalmers one day when she had asked him to wait behind to copy out extra words while she marked exercise books. 'I know that you're trying to help me, but it's not worth all this effort.'

'Oh yes, Cy,' she'd said gently. 'Yes, it is complicated and difficult, but it *is* worth the effort. Language is beautiful, it's versatile, compelling, and very wonderful.'

What's to be wonderful? thought Cy as he read

his dictionary definitions. He stumbled down the list, which included his first known meaning – a port by the sea – and then a type of wine – a drink, for heaven's sake! Cy's finger stopped as he found what he was looking for. 'Port – a gate or portal in a town or fortress: from the Latin *porta* – a gate.' Below that was: 'Portal – any entrance, gateway, or doorway, especially one that is large and impressive: from Latin *porta* – a gate.'

Cy felt quite pleased with himself. He decided to write it all down. It was bound to come in useful, if not for the volcano project, then certainly later in the term when they were studying the Romans.

Cy went back to the city plan. At the opposite end of the Via dell'Abbondanza was the Porta Marina. Now that last word he did know. A marina was to do with boats. He went back to his dictionary and found the word and its meaning – 'a docking facility' – so he guessed that the Porta Marina must be the gate which led to the harbour and the Mediterranean Sea. His eye wandered back along to the place where the road crossed the Via Stabiana. At the bottom of the map, near the Porta Stabia, were the barracks where the Dream Master at this very moment was waiting to fight for his life. Cy shivered. He let his eye follow the

Via Stabiana back up to the top of the map, where the road left the city – the road which headed inland and northwards towards the mighty city of Rome. The name of the gate leaped out from the page: 'Porta Vesuvio'.

'*Porta Vesuvio,*' Cy whispered.

He didn't need any dictionary to help him translate that. Vesuvius was the mountain in Italy which had once been an active volcano, a very active volcano. His grampa said it had been erupting when he was there during the Second World War. After the fighting in the Western Desert, Monty and Grampa had led the Eighth Army across the Mediterranean to Italy, and there, Grampa said, 'was old Vesuvio, crackling and thundering like nobody's business'. But it hadn't been such a huge explosion then. The most famous was ages earlier, in ancient times.

Cy wondered if Linus or Rhea Silvia would remember anything about it. How great would that be! He would have the best description in the whole class of a volcanic eruption if he could hear some first-hand accounts of what had happened! When he returned it would be the first thing that he would ask Linus. As Cy read a bit more a restless feeling began to come over him. It was a warm

August night but he drew the duvet cover around his shoulders.

There were drawings showing the volcano spouting fire, smoke and molten lava. Hot ash and deadly fumes were pouring down the hillsides. The eruption had been so vast and so awful that almost everyone had been killed. The city had been buried under the ash for centuries.

It must have happened *after* Linus and Rhea Silvia's life there, Cy reasoned, if the city had been covered over and lost for more than a thousand years. He remembered his conversation with Linus as they had taken the short cut at the Odeon to the gladiators' barracks. Linus had known of some kind of disaster at Pompeii, but it was not a volcanic eruption that Linus had spoken of, but an earthquake.

'They are still repairing buildings from the earthquake which happened many years ago,' Linus had said.

Then he had told Cy that he did not remember anything about the earthquake as it was before he was alive. It had happened the year Rhea Silvia was born.

Cy looked again at his book. It gave a few details about the earthquake at Pompeii and said that it

93

had happened in AD 62. Cy knew that Rhea Silvia was seventeen years old because he had heard her tell Lauren that this was her seventeenth summer.

Cy snapped the book shut, lay down in his bed and closed his eyes. His stomach was beginning those painful cramps that he knew so well, when events in life began to grow too big for him to handle. Now he knew that he *must* get back to Pompeii as soon as he could. This problem was so large that he dared not even *think* about it, let alone write it down.

If Rhea Silvia was seventeen years old and she had been born the year of the great earthquake in AD 62, then the year that she and her brother and the Dream Master were living in at Pompeii at this very moment was AD 79.

Cy kept his eyes pressed closed. He didn't need to look at the book again. The last sentence he had read was clear in his head:

In AD 79 the volcano Vesuvius erupted, killing most of the population and completely burying the town of Pompeii.

CHAPTER XII

The next morning at breakfast Cy's head was sore and he felt so tired and achy all over that he could hardly lift his spoon out of his cereal bowl. His dreams of the previous night, the normal everyday run-of-the-mill ones, had been confused and disturbing. He hadn't slept properly and he knew that he needed some mental rest so that he could cope with the problems to be dealt with when he was able to return to Pompeii.

Lauren was more grumpy than usual, and complaining about the warm weather. 'It's always the

same,' she moaned. 'The sun comes out as soon as the holidays are over.'

'I don't know what's the matter with the two of you,' said Cy's mum. 'Yesterday Lauren was mumping about here yawning her head off, and this morning you're as bad as she is, Cy.'

'By this time in the holidays they really need to be back at school,' said Cy's dad. 'They've not got enough to do, that's why they are both out of sorts.'

Cy scowled at his bowl of cereal. Every year at the end of the summer holidays either his mum or his dad *always* said something along the lines of 'I think you need something to occupy your minds: some school work would soon sort you out.' They claimed it was because they thought he and Lauren were bored. Cy suspected it was because his parents were fed up having them around the house all day. In the last week of the holidays they caught up with house-cleaning and decorating and Cy was sure that he and Lauren only got in their way.

'It's time you were back at school' was one of his most hated adult expressions, although it *was* true that he was a bit fed up. His school friends Vicky and Innis were away on holiday and Basra had family visiting from India. Grampa was staying with his other grandchildren, Cy's cousins, for a few weeks and Cy missed his company. If Grampa were here he'd have been able to advise Cy what to do about the Mean Machines.

'What are you doing today?'

Cy realized his mum was asking him a question. 'Doing . . . today.' Cy felt his brain do one of the slow slides it often did when he was asked a direct question. 'Ahhh . . .' he groped in his pocket and found the curtain ring Grampa had given him to help him remember things. His fingers connected with the piece of paper he had wrapped round it yesterday. It was a note of his Internet appointment! 'Library,' he mumbled through a mouthful of Oat Crunchies. 'School project work.'

'And you, Lauren?' Cy's mum turned to his sister.

Lauren rolled her eyes and ignored her mother.

Cy's dad caught Lauren's look. 'Is one allowed to enquire as to what plans you might have for today?' he asked in a sweet voice.

Lauren stood up and marched like a robot towards the door. Then she stopped and, staring straight ahead, she spoke in a monotone:

'I – am – now – going – out.

I – am – meeting – my – friend – Cartwheel.

We – will – go – to – the – house – of – our – friend – Baz.

Baz – and – Cartwheel – have – previously – been – cleared – for – close – contact – by – the Parents – division – of – the – FBI.

I – will – be – home – late – afternoon.

I – will – not – speak – to – strangers.

I – will – not – do – drugs.

I – will – not – imbibe – alcoholic – substances.

Goodbye.'

Lauren spun on her heel. The door crashed shut.

Cy's mum looked at his dad. 'I would *never* have spoken to my parents like that.'

'Let's look on it positively,' said Cy's dad. 'She didn't actually throw things.' He turned to Cy. 'Do you think you could do us a favour, old son? When you get to puberty, press the "skip" button.'

Cy's mum had picked up a large ring binder which lay on the kitchen table. It contained the notes for the modern language teachers' staff development course that she had been studying during her school holidays. 'Perhaps there's some-thing here that might help us with situations like these,' she said. 'I'm sure there was a whole section called "Aspects of Communication".'

'There hasn't yet been a course to cover the years of teenage carnage,' said Cy's dad. 'Whoever devises that module will become a millionaire. We'd be better off having a sign made up saying "HORMONE HAZARD ZONE" and pinning it on Lauren's bedroom door.'

'Wait!' Cy's mum pulled out a sheet of printed paper. 'Here's a bit about one-to-one responses. It says that not only should we listen and pay attention, we must also *tell* the person that we are doing this. And we must do so both in our body language and verbally. "Make eye contact. Let them know that they have your full attention. That you *notice* them and are listening *carefully*."' She glanced down at the course notes. '"Notice and listen carefully,"' she repeated under her breath. She looked over at Cy and then pulled her chair closer to his. 'I notice you,' she said.

Cy looked up from his breakfast.

Cy's mum locked eyes with him. 'I *notice* you carefully,' she said.

'What?' said Cy in alarm. His stomach dropped. He must have left some evidence of his trip to Pompeii lying about his room. 'What was it you noticed?'

'You,' said his mother, not taking her eyes from

Cy's face. 'I notice *you*. *You* have my full attention.'

'I don't want your full attention,' said Cy. 'Why are you always picking on me?' He got up and, slinging his rucksack over his shoulder, he went out of the kitchen, slamming the door behind him.

'I don't think I got that quite right,' he heard his mum tell his dad as he went down the path. 'Instead of "*notice* you carefully" perhaps I should have said "*carefully* notice you".'

When Cy reached the library the first two people that he saw were Eddie and Chloe. He had just entered the building and they were walking ahead of him. Whenever he met them Cy always felt slightly sick. He knew that Grampa gave good advice when he told him to try to ignore them, but Cy also knew that it took a lot of will-power to do that. It meant that he had to concentrate really hard on something else and he just wasn't up to it this morning.

Eddie and Chloe went past the front desk and straight along to the computer area. Cy almost turned at once to go away. But as he hesitated, the librarian spotted him and waved him over to his computer terminal.

'I'll log on for you and if you give me an idea

what you're looking for I can point you in the right direction.'

Cy nodded his thanks. He was only half listening. The Mean Machines were further down the library and Cy couldn't help but let his gaze wander towards them while the librarian was busy logging onto the terminal for him. Despite his best intentions his eyes appeared to have a will of their own. Cy watched Eddie and Chloe stop and put their bags on the floor. The two bullies sat down close to another computer terminal where someone else was working. Cy recognized Vojek, a younger boy who had only come to his school last term. Cy wondered what the Mean Machines were up to. Suddenly Eddie looked up and saw Cy staring. At once Eddie nudged Chloe. Chloe turned her head and glared.

Cy dropped his eyes, but it was too late. He had been spotted! The Mean Machines had seen him!

CHAPTER XIII

Cy felt a great wave of nausea sweep up from his stomach. He swallowed carefully, trying to hold onto his Oat Crunchies. Eddie and Chloe stared at him for a long, long moment . . . and then an amazing thing happened. Chloe shook her head. She pointed at Vojek. The Mean Machines had found a new victim.

Cy felt his muscles slowly relax and he began to breathe. They weren't after him today. It was someone else's turn.

'That's all set up.'

Cy turned his head. The librarian was speaking to him.

'There's a few good websites on volcanoes. I've bookmarked them for you. I've got some work to attend to so I'll leave you to browse but you can let me know if you need any help.'

Cy sat down and began his Internet search. There was a bewildering amount of information on volcanoes. Ones that exploded, ones that poured lava, ones that were under the sea – the largest of all was the one in outer space! Cy made lots of notes and then began his search for information about the eruption at Pompeii.

He found an extract of a report written at the time by a Roman known as Pliny the Younger who had actually seen it happening from across the bay. He wrote of a column of smoke and a strange dark cloud which blotted out the sun. It had started in the late morning of 24 August and, by present-day reckoning, the year had been AD 79. There had been minor earth tremors before the first eruption occurred. But it wasn't the eruptions of showers of rock or the hot ash that killed so many of the citizens. It was the scorching gas that came some hours after this, travelling at a terrifying speed. The volcano was nine miles from Pompeii, but within minutes of the gas clouds racing down the mountainside thousands of people had suffocated.

Cy looked at the photographs of the archaeological site that was now Pompeii. He could see the ruins of the Via dell'Abbondanza, of the Amphitheatre, of the Barracks of the Gladiators. The streets he had run along with Linus – they had all been destroyed in a matter of hours.

The top of the mountain had exploded around midday and for twelve hours rocks, ash and pumice had fallen on people and buildings like hot hailstones. Then the great towering pillar of smoke had collapsed and – Cy wrote the phrase out carefully in his notebook – the *pyroclastic flow* had come racing down the mountain and nothing could withstand it.

Cy decided to print the pages and then go. He was worried about leaving the Dream Master so long without his dreamcloak. And something about the description of the destruction of Pompeii was disturbing him, but he didn't quite know why.

As he got up, Cy noticed that Vojek was hunched in his seat, trying to take up as small a space as possible. Cy looked around. Eddie and Chloe must have eventually stopped annoying him and gone on into the Reference section. But

Vojek still sat on in his own misery. The younger boy had pulled his head and neck down into his shoulders, curled like a snail in its shell. Cy remembered what it was like to be picked on at that age. He looked at Vojek and saw himself.

There was something wrong. But it was none of his business, Cy decided. He had his own problems: the Dream Master to rescue, his school work to do, and anyway, he especially did not want to go looking for trouble with Eddie and Chloe. Vojek would need to look after himself – just as Cy did . . .

Except that he didn't – not totally, anyway. Cy's friends Vicky, Basra and Innis often backed him up and he had his grampa to talk to. Who did Vojek have? He tried to remember what Mrs Chalmers had said about welcoming those fleeing persecution, and how we should try to help them in any way we could. But it was difficult to do this. The families who had sought asylum in the town knew very little of the English language.

Cy thought about language and how it helped make life easier. He thought about his sister Lauren and her friends and the crazy text messages they sent each other on their mobile phones. How easy it was for them to do this and have fun because they knew what the letters meant. When he travelled with the dreamcloak it didn't seem to matter. In some way he understood the language and Linus and Rhea Silvia understood his. What must it be like *not* to understand? And not in the way a very young child doesn't understand – when you were tiny you were too little to know about things. But Vojek *did* know. He would have been able to speak and laugh in his own land. Now he would realize that he was prevented from studying or even playing properly in this country.

Cy walked slowly across the library, paused and looked at Vojek's computer. The screen was showing gobbledegook. Vojek kept his head down.

Cy gently touched his shoulder. When the younger boy looked up, Cy pointed to himself and said, 'Cy. My name is Cy.'

'Vojek,' the younger boy mumbled. 'Name Vojek.'

Cy indicated the screen. 'What's this?'

'Lit-er-acy.' Vojek spoke carefully. 'I try to learn English.'

Not from that, you won't, thought Cy. Something was malfunctioning, or . . . of course! The Mean Machines! It would be just like them to fiddle about and mess up Vojek's program.

Cy pointed to the computer and then to the Reference section. He made signs with his hands. 'Did Eddie and Chloe touch your machine?'

'Yes,' Vojek whispered. He looked fearfully over his shoulder, and then jumped in alarm. The librarian was standing behind them.

'What's the problem?'

'The keyboard's frozen,' said Cy, 'and the mouse isn't working either.'

The librarian looked at the screen. 'I put on a CD with a basic literacy program. You've changed the settings,' she said to Vojek.

Vojek said nothing.

'I don't think he did,' said Cy.

'But he must have,' said the librarian. She tutted. 'You kids. This is the best equipment and it's put here to help you. If you muck around with it, it'll just get broken.' She closed down the program and switched the computer off. Then she reached over and swivelled the machine round. 'These serial ports have been changed over. What you've done here,' she said crossly, 'is actually dangerous!'

Vojek gave a terrified little moan. 'No! No! No trouble. No trouble. My mother afraid . . . if trouble.'

Cy looked at the fear in Vojek's eyes. Mrs

Chalmers had told her class that Vojek's parents had brought their family here to be safe. His father had been a doctor who had tried to treat patients from both sides of the conflict in their own country.

'I appreciate that a lot of things must be very strange for you here,' said the librarian, 'but you must know that you should not interfere with the back of the machines. You could hurt yourself, and also you might not be allowed to use it again.'

'Yes. Thank you,' said Vojek.

Cy stared at him. Vojek was prepared to take the blame because he was afraid of trouble. He had come to this country looking for freedom from fear, and right away that freedom was being taken from him.

Cy knew what it was like to be afraid to speak up. But if he couldn't speak up for himself, then maybe he could do it for another. He must. He could. He would.

'Vojek didn't touch the back of the machine.'

'Was it you then?' The librarian was busy unplugging the serial ports and re-connecting the keyboard and mouse.

'It wasn't Vojek, and it wasn't me.' Cy pretended to look puzzled. 'I suppose it must have been someone else.'

The librarian gave him a blank look. 'It was working when I set it up and there are only the two of you here at the moment.'

'Perhaps earlier?' suggested Cy. 'When I arrived, weren't there a couple of people walking through here?'

The librarian snapped her fingers. 'There were those two youngsters who were capering about yesterday. They came in immediately before you and went to the Reference section. Do you know their names?'

Cy felt a bit queasy. He hesitated. It was the most awful thing to do – to tell on someone. Then he saw Vojek's small anxious face watching him. 'Eddie and Chloe,' said Cy. 'They stopped at Vojek's desk and were fiddling about while you were busy logging on my terminal.'

'I'll just go and have a word with them,' said the librarian. 'I'm not prepared to allow someone to vandalize equipment and let another person take the blame.' She had a very determined look in her eye.

Cy stood in front of her. 'It was fortunate that you happened to be passing and saw Eddie and Chloe change the serial ports,' he said firmly.

'I didn't, Cy, it was you,' said the librarian.

'No,' said Cy emphatically. 'It was you.'

The librarian gave him a puzzled look. 'It was you. You just told me about it not two minutes ago.'

Cy did not take his eyes from her face. 'It – was – you,' he said with finality.

As the librarian began to open her mouth, Vojek plucked at her sleeve. 'Cy no tell-tale,' he whispered.

'Whaaat?' The librarian looked at the younger boy and then at Cy. 'Oh . . . oh I see. Yes, of course.' She spoke slowly. 'Let me get this right. I looked over at this computer terminal to see how Vojek was getting on and I noticed Eddie and Chloe tampering with the back of the machine. This was when they stopped here before going into the Reference section . . . which I saw them doing.' She smiled at Cy and Vojek. 'Would that be what happened?'

Cy nodded.

'Good,' said the librarian. 'I think I'll go now and have a word with those two.' She set off briskly towards the Reference section.

Cy went to collect his material from the printer. He deliberately turned his back so that he would not see any rude signs or gestures that Eddie and

110

Chloe might make at him as they left the library. Cy knew that the Mean Machines were not finished with him or Vojek or any number of other people. They would go on and on, picking on those who were vulnerable. Some people were like that. They seemed to take pleasure in annoying other people or making them unhappy. If it wasn't Eddie and Chloe doing it, it could easily be someone else. There would always be another bully to take their place. Cy had to find his own way of coping with them, him and Vojek . . .

Cy glanced over to where the small figure of Vojek had sat earlier, crouched low over his mouse-mat. Except that Vojek's shoulders weren't hunched any more. He was sitting up straight and flicking happily through his literacy learning program. He saw Cy looking at him and smiled.

When the asylum-seekers had first come to the area, the librarian had put up flash cards with foreign language phrases all over the library. Cy wandered about until he found one in Croatian. He looked down the list until he found a suitable greeting and then, carefully following the pronunciation guide, he called across to Vojek.

'*Vidimo se!* See you later, Vojek.'

The younger boy looked up in happy surprise.

111

'*Vidimo se!*' he replied. '*Vidimo se.*'

After sorting and stapling his computer print-out Cy left the library. He was happier than he had been this morning. His Internet search had given him enough information about volcanoes to write up his school project, and he also knew a great deal more about Pompeii. As soon as he got back home he would try to return to ancient Roman times and rescue the Dream Master. He and the Dream Master could persuade Rhea Silvia and Linus to join their parents at the family's mosaic workshops in Rome for the remainder of the summer. Then the two young people would be far away from Pompeii and safe from any eruption from Vesuvius. Cy was whistling as he opened the kitchen door.

'I'm starving. What's for lunch?'

'At least one of our children is speaking to us,' said Cy's dad to his mum. He had a paintbrush in his hand and was perched on a ladder, painting the kitchen window-frames.

Cy's mum was dragging wet clothes from the washing machine. 'I've stopped the laundry in mid-wash,' she said. 'I'll need to take a look at the washing machine. When that last load was in, the machine was whining in the weirdest way. It almost sounded as though someone was trapped in there.'

Cy glanced across at the soggy bundle piled up at his mother's feet. The old beach towel he had taken from the linen cupboard outside his bedroom lay soaking wet and crumpled on the floor. On it and through it ran a filmy squelchy gooey grey mess.

Cy staggered as if he'd been struck across the face. Lying on the kitchen floor, utterly drained of energy, was his Dream Master's dreamcloak!

CHAPTER XIV

'W hat have you *done*!'
Cy's voice was trembling so much that he couldn't go on. He kneeled down beside the dreamcloak. The strange substance shivered and seemed to weep around him.

'I . . . I . . .' Cy's mum was a bit shaken. 'I was sorting clothes, looking out warmer things for the autumn, and I found this under your bed.'

'I keep my own stuff under my bed right at the back!' shouted Cy. 'Can't I get any privacy in this house?'

'Of course you can.' Cy's mum tried to put her arm round his shoulder but Cy threw it off. 'I'm sorry. I thought it was just some old clothes you'd worn on the beach.'

'You've ruined it,' said Cy. He was almost crying. 'It'll never work again. It's destroyed.'

Cy's father came down the ladder to have a look.

'What is it anyway?' asked Cy's mum.

'It's obvious,' said Cy's dad.

Cy's heart jumped. He looked up at his father.

'Cy told you. It's one of his experiments. Probably to do with his school project.' Cy's dad kneeled down. 'Look, son, why don't you put this ... um ... put this away under your bed. No-one will touch it again.' He glanced at Cy's mum.

She nodded. 'Come back down when you've done that,' she said. 'I'll make some cool milk shakes.'

Cy gathered the ends of the towel and wrapped up the remains of the dreamcloak. He went slowly upstairs and shoved it back under his bed. He sat for a minute or two, but he knew that he would have to go downstairs again and allow his parents to make it up to him. Otherwise they would only come to his room and try to have a meaningful conversation with him about emotions, relationships or growing up.

In the kitchen Cy found his father looking through the cupboards.

'Right, Cy, I've got it.' His dad held up a tiny bottle of dark liquid.

Cy sat down and began to drink the milk shake that his mum had made him. 'What?' he asked.

'Cochineal. Red food colouring. And don't worry,' Cy's dad added, as he saw the expression on Cy's face. 'We are not going to bake.'

'What are we going to do?'

'Make a volcano.' Cy's dad lifted the kettle full of hot water. 'Could you put some cold water in a bowl and bring it outside, please, Cy? When you've finished your milk shake. I'll find the rest of the stuff we need in the hut.'

Cy trailed after his father into the garden.

'I thought showing you this might help with your project.'

Cy watched as his dad rummaged around in the garden hut. There is so much stuff in here, thought Cy, he can't possibly know where everything is. His dad took an old cardboard box and cut out a square from one side. Then he punched a small hole in the centre with a nail. He found some corks from when he had tried wine-making after a family visit to France. Then he dug out a glass jam jar and a small narrow-necked bottle. He took all the bits and pieces and placed them on the garden table.

'We'll put a few drops of food colouring in this narrow-necked bottle and fill it up with warm water from the kettle. That's the cone of the volcano.'

Cy's dad half filled the jam jar with cold water from the basin and placed the pierced square of card on the top. Then he upended the jar and card onto the top of the small bottle with the red-coloured liquid. He waited a few moments and then began to press down carefully. Slowly, little drifts of colour began to seep through the hole in the card. As Cy watched they rose upwards in spurts through the cold water.

'Do you know why that is happening?' asked Cy's dad, and then he answered before Cy could reply. 'It's because warm liquid rises!'

Cy watched the tiny puffs of red and imagined that they were fire and hot rock hurtling into the air.

'Just think of what that would be like magnified a thousand million times,' said Cy's dad. 'The magma chamber of the volcano is full of molten rock. It tries to push up through the earth's crust to escape. When it does come through the surface then it becomes rivers of lava flowing away from the vents. Sometimes the magma is not so runny. It can be so hard that it blocks the upward flow of the gases behind it.'

Cy's dad took some of the corks and held them under the water in the basin. 'These gases are deadly and they build up until there is an enormous explosion.' He released the corks and they shot to the surface of the water. 'It creates a huge, intensely hot poisonous cloud of ash and gas. That's called a pyroclastic surge.'

It was a hot August afternoon but Cy shivered. He knew from his research this morning that the explosive kinds of volcanic eruption were the most dangerous. The force that had blown the top off Mount St Helens had blasted eight thousand million tonnes of rock into the air. Cy also knew that people living near these types of volcano often had little or no warning of what was about to happen.

Cy's dad lifted the model and took it into the house. Cy's mum had the insides of the washing machine spread out on the floor and was kneeling amongst them, studying the operating manual. Cy's dad leaned over to show her the volcano experiment.

'Look at that,' he said. 'It demonstrates the scientific principles of volcanic eruptions.' He set the model down on the worktop and gazed at it. 'I'm quite proud of that,' he said.

Cy's mum looked up from the floor. 'The kitchen window-frames are only half-painted,' she said tersely.

'I was spending quality time with my son,' said Cy's dad. 'You don't begrudge us that, do you?'

Cy's mum glared at his dad. 'I'm glad that you've got time for amusing yourself.'

Cy began to edge towards the door.

'You were the one talking this morning about establishing good communication,' said Cy's dad. 'I don't call it "amusing myself". I look on it as positive parenting.'

'Right,' said Cy's mum. 'I think it's fairly straightforward to make models with children. How about you do something really challenging?'

'I don't think that there is any aspect of parenting where I am not prepared to have a go at least,' said Cy's dad in an aggrieved voice.

'Really?' said Cy's mum. She beamed a benign smile, but her eyes showed triumph.

Oho, Dad, thought Cy, you should have been more careful. He recognized his mum's look. If you were playing chess, it was the one that you saw on your opponent's face just before they said, 'Checkmate.'

'Tell you what, darling.' His mum's tone, although soft, had an edge to it. 'Tomorrow you can go shopping with Lauren to purchase her new school skirt.'

There was a long pause.

'Ah,' Cy heard his dad say as he slipped quietly out of the kitchen.

CHAPTER XV

'WHERE IS MY DREAMCLOAK!!!!!!!!!!'
The Dream Master was apoplectic.
He flung himself against the door of
his cubicle in the gladiators' barracks, spitting
flecks of foam over his beard.

'At home,' said Cy nervously.

'Why is it not here?'

'Er, it was my mum's fault actually,' said Cy.

'What?'

'My mum,' said Cy. 'I put the dreamcloak under
my bed. Right at the back. I thought it would be

safe there. She decided to sort out clothes. So she took it out from under the bed and—'

The Dream Master thrust his hand through the bars of his cell and grabbed Cy by the neck. 'Tell me *exactly* where my dreamcloak is, at this precise moment. Now!'

'It's under my bed.'

'I thought you said your mother had it.'

'She did, but I got it back.'

'But you just said it was her fault that you have not brought it with you.'

'It is.' Cy took a deep, deep breath and spoke as quickly as he could. 'She thought it looked a bit grubby and a little rinse through would smarten it up.'

'What are you talking about?'

'The washing machine.'

'The washing machine?'

Cy loosened the Dream Master's hold on his neck and stepped back from the cell door. 'My mum put your dreamcloak in the washing.'

'WHAAAAAAAAAAAT?!'

The little man stamped his foot so hard that one of his greaves fell off. 'You allowed your mother to put my dreamcloak in a washing machine?'

'She used fabric softener,' said Cy.

'I don't care what she used!' bawled the Dream Master. 'You just don't put a dreamcloak in a washing machine. It's completely disrespectful! My dreamcloak has survived Fire, Flood and Famine. My dreamcloak has taken me through the Red Sea, the Dead Sea and across the Sea of Tranquillity. I've walked on the Great Wall of China and swum off the Great Barrier Reef. My dreamcloak . . .' His voice tailed off.

'I'm really sorry,' said Cy.

The Dream Master sat down and put his head in his hands. 'I should have known it would be the twenty-first century that would harm my precious dreamcloak. The people who live in this Time have no idea about *anything*.' He glared at Cy. 'Your mother puts it in a washing machine and you think, you Nit-witted Numpty, that adding fabric softener might help?'

'I got it out after only a few minutes,' said Cy. 'I think it can be fixed.' He paused. 'That's something I've always wanted to ask you. The energy in the dreamcloak – where does it come from? Where is the centre?'

'Not "where",' said the Dream Master. '"Who".'

'Who,' repeated Cy. 'Who?'

'You're beginning to sound like an owl,' said the

Dream Master. 'A fact I find worrying, as I am now relying on you to re-unite me with my dreamcloak. You who can barely tell a story without using a cliché!'

'A cliché?' said Cy.

'A cliché,' said the Dream Master nastily. 'You know. An expression that has lost its meaning through being employed too often.'

'Does that include alliteration?' Cy asked equally nastily. 'I can't tell you how many times you use alliteration.'

'Alliteration is *good*,' said the Dream Master. 'That's imaginative use of language.'

'My *adjectives* are good,' said Cy. 'Mrs Chalmers told me that they were very expressive.'

'That's another thing that everyone overuses,' said the Dream Master. 'Adjectives are absolutely knackered.'

'Isn't *that* an adjective?' asked Cy.

'Don't push it,' said the Dream Master. 'You are supposed to have a good Imagination. Just think of how exhausting it would be if you were an adjective. Do you have any idea how many millions of people on millions of computers every day type out the word 'nice'. Do you have the slightest conception of how many trees have been sacrificed to make pencils, of the oceans of ink that have been squandered so that humans can overuse adjectives?'

'What are we supposed to do?' demanded Cy.

'Verbs, you Vacant Vagrant. Verbs . . . That's what they are there for. They are the "being" words and the "doing" words.'

'I know about verbs,' said Cy. 'I use verbs.'

'Yes, but do you choose any verb, or the easiest, or the first one that pops into your head?'

'Why not?' asked Cy.

'Because people who do that begin to shove in adverbs all over the place. Something you may have noticed yourself doing,' the Dream Master said sarcastically.

'Adverbs are there to support the verb,' said Cy. 'Mrs Chalmers told the class that. I can give you lots of examples.'

'We are not going there,' said the Dream Master.

Cy thought about it. He recalled being in the library when he had spoken gently to Vojek, and then firmly and emphatically to the librarian. Maybe he did overuse adverbs. But then . . . the librarian had walked off briskly, and Cy was sure that, generally speaking, librarians knew what they were doing. 'When used *properly* in the context of the story, adverbs contribute *positively* to the verb,' said Cy. 'And I'm saying that very *firmly*,' he added.

The Dream Master gave him an odd look. 'Does this mean that you are now able to take proper command of this dream? Would you, for instance, be able to make this locked door disappear?' He waited. Then he kicked his cell door. 'I thought not,' he said. 'Can I also ask why it has taken you two days to get back here?'

'I had a bit of difficulty with the dreamsilk,' Cy admitted, 'which held me up for a couple of days.' He'd tell the Dream Master later about what had happened to him as he'd boomeranged about in TimeSpace . . . much later. 'I still need practice.'

'So,' said the Dream Master, 'bring out your piece of dreamsilk and let's attempt to leave ancient Pompeii.'

'Ahh . . .' said Cy. 'We need to talk about that.'

'What's to talk about? Use your piece of dream-silk and let's go.'

'No,' said Cy. He held his hand up as the Dream Master began to speak. 'Listen. This is AD seventy-nine. It is the year Vesuvius erupted and buried Pompeii. I am not leaving until I warn some people about what will happen.'

The Dream Master gave Cy a grave look. 'You cannot change history.'

'I know,' said Cy. 'I have thought about that. But at least I might be able to persuade Linus and Rhea Silvia to leave.'

'You might not be able to.'

'I must try.'

'What must you try?' asked a voice.

Cy turned. Linus was standing behind him. 'I have been looking for you for some time. You should not have come down here without me,' he scolded Cy.

Cy bowed his head.

'But I am glad you did. Today is the holiday, and we can go to the Amphitheatre now and secure a good seat.' Linus saluted the Dream Master. 'I wish you well.'

Before either the Dream Master or Cy could reply they heard the sound of marching footsteps approaching.

'They are coming for you,' said Linus. 'It is time for you to fight.'

CHAPTER XVI

'Slaves may not sit with their masters,' Linus told Cy as they entered the Amphitheatre. He put his hand on Cy's arm. 'Try not to worry too much about your friend. It is an honourable way to die.'

Cy shuddered. Linus bought some food to eat during the games and then Cy left him in a seat in the shaded part of the Amphitheatre. Cy walked round the huge stadium, pushing his way through the crowds until he was standing close to the parapet at the gladiators' entrance. Behind him the

tiered stone and wooden seats were filling up
rapidly as the citizens of Pompeii came to see the
new fighter, whose famous bad temper was now
being talked about all over town.

Cy shaded his eyes against the rising sun and
watched as, led by an Indian elephant and two
camels, the procession of the gladiators entered the
ring. The little figure of the Dream Master was in
the lead. Cy signalled desperately as the column of
animals and figures circled the great ellipse of the
arena. Eventually the Dream Master caught sight
of him and gestured that he had seen Cy. The procession wound its way back outside. There was a
long intermission when people queued to place
bets and buy food and drink. Then the first combat
was announced.

Following a loud fanfare of trumpets, the master
of the games stood up and cried out, 'First for
today, I now present to you the most famous, the
most skilful, the most courageous ... Dominus
Somniorum!'

Cy's tongue clamped itself to the roof of his
mouth in fright as the Dream Master stepped into
the blinding sun of the Amphitheatre. The roar
from the crowd almost lifted him off his feet.

'What are they saying?' the little man shouted

up at Cy. He twisted his head this way and that in his helmet. 'I can hardly hear or see inside this piece of tin!'

'They are shouting for you,' said Cy.

'*Dominus Somniorum! Dominus Somniorum!*' chanted the crowd.

'Is there anyone else in the arena?' asked the Dream Master.

'No,' said Cy, 'but—'

'Sometimes you have to be firm with people,' said the Dream Master. 'I told them that I would not fight and they have honoured my wishes.' He strutted forwards, waved his sword high above his head and acknowledged the applause of the spectators. He bowed to each section of the Amphitheatre, then he laid his sword down. 'Can I go now?' he asked.

The crowd roared in delight. Cy looked at the people next to him who were cheering and applauding. They thought the little man was showing great spirit! They thought the Dream Master was choosing unarmed combat!

A rattling noise echoed around the Amphitheatre. The crowd fell silent. In the far wall a gridded iron gate scraped open. From the dark-ness beyond, a full-grown African lion leaped slashing and snarling out into the sand.

Cy hurriedly reached under his sweatshirt for the bundle he had hidden there. 'Run!' he shouted at the Dream Master. 'Over here! Run!'

The little man didn't need to be told twice. He scuttled as fast as he could towards Cy's side of the arena. 'I hope you have a plan!' he yelled.

Cy's heart was going so fast that he thought he was going to fall over. 'It's all I could think of!' he yelled back and threw down the items that he had taken from the garden hut at home.

'Three Roman candles, a crackerjack and two sparklers? This is supposed to save my life?' wailed the Dream Master.

'The matches! Don't forgot to pick up the matches!' Cy shouted. 'And try to act brave. Linus says the people favour a brave fighter, and it is they who can decide your fate.'

It was fortunate indeed that the people had taken the new little gladiator known as Dominus Somniorum to their hearts. Not only did they view his relinquishing his sword as an act of immense courage; they had also placed a large amount of money on him to win. As the lion approached the Dream Master, sensing an easy if not very nourishing meal, the crowd began to pelt it with any object they could lay their hands on. While the little man fumbled about trying to strike a match to set off the fireworks, an assortment of jars, coins, bottles, sandals and stones bounced off the animal's body. The lion stopped in confusion and shook its head from side to side.

Then Cy had a terrific idea. He grabbed a tray from one of the vendors, raced round inside the arena and dropped the food at the opening to the animal's cage. There was a muttering from the crowd. Cy swallowed, his throat dry. Would they think this was cheating?

Suddenly a small figure stood up and shouted, 'Hurrah! Victory to Dominus Somniorum!'

Cy looked across the Amphitheatre. At the opposite side, beyond the parapet brightly painted with hunting scenes and pictures of former contests, he saw Linus climb onto his seat and hurl his own food at the open door of the *bestiarii*.

The spectators screamed their approval and rushed to follow his example. There was a near riot as bread, fruit, cheese and kebabs of all kinds rained down into the arena. By this time the Dream Master had managed to light some of the fireworks. He stood in a circle of effervescing Roman candles, holding a sparkler in each hand. The lion backed away from the fire and loped to where it could smell a dinner that did not fight back.

'That was the most unusual fight I've ever seen,' said Linus as the three of them left the Amphitheatre. 'Although, in Pompeii we are famed for disorder at our games. In former days crowd behaviour was so bad that the Roman Senate banned us from holding any spectacles at all in the Amphitheatre.' He looked at the Dream Master in admiration. 'You were very brave, facing the lion without using your sword. It is not surprising that you were granted your freedom.'

'I have wide experience in all kinds of situations,' said the Dream Master. 'It didn't take me long to work out a way to outwit that beast.'

Cy was too busy thinking of how he could persuade Rhea Silvia and Linus to leave the town to challenge the truth of the Dream Master's words. If their mother had gone to join their father in Rome, perhaps he could pretend that she had sent for their children to join them? But then there was the problem of how they would travel to Rome. They could not be expected to walk, and he had no money to hire a chariot. Perhaps their father owned a wagon and they could use that? Cy's mind was still searching through possibilities when, deep below the cobbles of the street, he heard a faint low rumble like an underground train.

'What was that?' he asked.

'Thunder,' said Linus.

'It seemed to come from below us,' said Cy. 'And anyway there are no rain clouds.'

'The bay is wide and summer storms come in very fast from the sea.' Linus glanced up at the sky. 'See,' he said, 'the clouds are coming our way now.'

Cy looked upwards. Faint plumes of feathery grey were drifting across the sky. He frowned. 'Those clouds are not blowing in from the sea,' he said to Linus, 'they are coming from the mountains.'

Linus halted in the street and faced the hills. 'You are right,' he said. 'How strange.'

As they spoke the ground shuddered again beneath their feet.

Linus's eyes opened wide in fear. 'It is a god within the earth turning in his sleep.'

'It is more likely to be an earthquake,' said the Dream Master.

'Then that is not such a worry,' said Linus. He

started to walk along the road again, with Cy and the Dream Master following. 'We often have tremors in the hot summer months.'

Cy had not spoken for several moments. He had been studying the odd greyish clouds which were trailing steadily over their heads. They did not look at all like clouds, not even bad-weather clouds. They looked more like ... Cy suddenly recalled his next-door neighbour's bonfire. He turned his head away from Linus and whispered quietly to the Dream Master. 'The date,' he said. 'Do you know today's date?'

'Well, really!' the Dream Master tutted. 'I have just escaped being eaten by a lion and might now be threatened with an earthquake, and you want to know the date?'

'The date,' said Cy, still quietly but more insistently. 'It is very important. What is today's date?'

'How could I forget it?' The little man was huffing and puffing to keep up with Cy, who had begun to walk faster. 'I will remember it for ever as the date I fought a savage beast,' he said. 'It is the twenty-fourth of August.'

Cy stopped so suddenly that the Dream Master, who was walking close behind, cannoned into him.

'Seneca and Caesar!' shouted the little man, holding his nose. 'What's the matter now?'

Cy grabbed the Dream Master by both shoulders and spoke in a low urgent voice. 'That is not cloud in the sky. It is smoke! This year is AD seventy-nine and August the twenty-fourth is the very day that the volcano in Vesuvius erupted, burying the town of Pompeii and everyone in it.'

CHAPTER XVII

Cy turned to speak to Linus, but the Dream Master pulled him back.

'Wait a moment,' he said. 'If Vesuvius is about to erupt, why don't we all just leave?'

'My dreamsilk is quite faded,' said Cy. 'It took a great deal of effort for me to get back to this precise TimeSpace so that I could rescue you. I was wandering about all over for Ages. I'm not very good at focusing, you know that.'

'But your piece of dreamsilk is not *completely* faded,' the Dream Master persisted.

Cy nodded in agreement. 'Not totally, no.'

'So therefore ...' The Dream Master's eyes seemed to see into Cy's very soul. '*You* could leave. There is enough energy in your scrap of dreamsilk to get *you* out of here.'

'What would happen to Rhea Silvia and Linus?' asked Cy. He felt his mind swivel as he considered the alternative ways that he could act. It seemed such a *reasonable* thing to do, to look after himself. After all, it wasn't his problem and he could end up in danger if he went to help someone else. And anyway, in life everybody should learn to cope on their own.

Then Cy remembered how Linus had risen to help him in the Amphitheatre. He remembered Vojek in the library. People weren't just on their own. Sometimes things that you did had a direct effect on other people, their lives, their happiness. Although there were some things that you had to do by yourself ... like making this decision. And now he, Cy, was in that position. He didn't have anyone like Grampa to discuss it with.

Cy met the Dream Master's eyes and shook his head. 'I am staying to help them,' he said.

'So, get on with it,' the Dream Master said grumpily.

Cy took Linus by the hand. 'We must move fast.' The air was tense and another tremor vibrated through the city. People had begun to hurry indoors. The smoky clouds above them thickened and a steady stream of hot hail began to fall from the sky.

'Is it an earthquake, like the one seventeen years ago?' asked Linus as he ran with Cy towards his home.

'This has never happened before,' said Cy. 'It is not an earthquake.'

Rhea Silvia came hurrying from the house to meet them. 'There are people coming into the city from the countryside. They say that the vineyards are on fire!'

'We must leave,' said Cy. 'We must leave *now*. Find something to cover our heads.'

Linus brought togas for himself and the Dream Master and Cy to wrap themselves in. Rhea Silvia took a cushion and, using Lauren's school tie, she tied it around her head.

As they stood in the street, unsure which way to turn, Cy bent and picked up one of the stones which had fallen from the sky. It was so hot that he could hardly hold it in his hand. The force of the eruption had blasted this rock across many miles.

139

It was greyish white and not very heavy at all. He examined it carefully. The stone was pitted with cavities, almost as though it was full of air bubbles.

That was what made it so lightweight, thought Cy as he studied the rock in his hand. A word shot into his brain. 'Pumice,' he said. He remembered his father's volcanic demonstration in the garden. At this very moment, deep in the magma chamber of Vesuvius, it wasn't just air that was building up pressure, it was noxious gases heating to a frighteningly high temperature.

Rhea Silvia looked at the grey ash which was now pouring from the sky. 'I have changed my mind,' she said. 'I think we should stay indoors.'

'I don't think that is a good idea,' said Cy.

Rhea and Linus exchanged glances. 'How would a slave know what is or what is not a good idea?' demanded Rhea Silvia.

'It is not a minor eruption,' said Cy. 'These falling rocks and ash are not so dangerous. It is what will come after.'

'We have friends in Herculaneum,' said Linus. 'We could go there.'

'No,' said Cy. 'Not Herculaneum.'

'Why not?' asked Rhea Silvia.

'The lava flow,' said Cy desperately. 'The red-hot lava flow will come down the mountainside. It will make a river of boiling mud and Herculaneum is directly in its path.'

'I don't understand how is it that you know so much about volcanoes,' said Linus. 'My father told me that Britain has no earthquakes or volcanoes. He said that the weather is very mild.'

Rhea Silvia and Linus both stared at Cy with a questioning look.

'I just know—' Cy began, and then he stopped. He was doing to Rhea Silvia and Linus the very thing that he hated adults doing to him – not explaining. Cy knew how frustrating it was to be told something with no explanation. Adults frequently did this by saying, 'I just know.' It was how they avoided difficult situations. But Cy always felt better when he knew *why* he was doing something. Linus and Rhea Silvia, although separated from his twenty-first-century TimeSpace by two thousand years, probably felt exactly the same. Cy looked at their faces and realized that they were both terrified.

'Listen,' he said gently. 'I am going to take a few seconds to explain this to you. My father is very learned, and has studied the movements of the earth and has told me all about it. Below the earth is a great fire.'

Linus nodded. 'Yes, it is the forge of the great god Vulcan.'

'Helped by the one-eyed Cyclops,' added Rhea Silvia.

'My father,' Cy went on, 'is a famous man of science. In Britain he is well known for his knowledge in these matters.'

'And what would he say in these circumstances?' asked Rhea Silvia.

'He would say that the noise you hear, and the smoke and ash you see, are from the great fire burning underground. He would also say that the mountain cannot hold back the fire for very much longer, and very soon Vesuvius will explode. He would tell us to go far away from here as quickly as we can.'

Rhea Silvia and Linus nodded. 'Yes,' said Rhea Silvia, 'we understand.'

'The volcano will not wait,' said Cy. 'Not until help comes, nor until you have reached safety. It will throw out flames and molten rock which will reach high above us. After a time this great pillar of smoke will collapse and then the searing hot air will rush down on top of us. Anyone who breathes it cannot live.' Cy tried to remember the name he had written down from his Internet search: Pie . . . pie-something.

'Pyroclastic surge,' murmured a voice in his ear.

'Could we outrun it?' asked Linus.

'No,' said Cy. 'We must be many miles from here when it happens. When it comes, it will travel faster than your best horseman on his fastest horse.'

CHAPTER XVIII

'My father's chariot!' cried Linus. 'It is kept with the innkeeper in the next street.'

'I will collect a few things for the journey,' said Rhea Silvia. She made to re-enter the house.

Cy tugged at her sleeve. 'There is not enough time and we must carry nothing. Soak some cloths in water from the fountain in the courtyard while Linus and I get the chariot ready.'

When they returned, Rhea Silvia, who had spoken to some women passing in the street, said,

'There is word that the admiral of the fleet himself is coming to rescue us.'

Cy recalled his Internet search and the print-out of Pliny the Younger's letter. 'They will not be able to land,' said Cy. 'The wind is too strong and it is blowing offshore.'

'Where can we go?' asked Rhea Silvia in despair.

'Towards the sea,' said Cy, hoping that he sounded as though he knew what he was doing. 'That's our best chance.'

Standing in the chariot with Linus by his side, Cy shortened the reins on the two horses. He tried to recall the map of Pompeii. In which direction lay the sea?

Beside him Linus was trembling in fear. Behind him Rhea Silvia, protected by the Dream Master, was crouched low in the chariot, trying to avoid the masonry and roof tiles which were cascading from the buildings.

As Cy hesitated, the horses made the decision for him. Spooked by the noise and the atmosphere, they began to trot nervously down the road. Cy could see the map of Pompeii in his mind's eye – the long straight lines of the roads laid out in the typical manner of a Roman town. And around it was the city wall with gates ... of course! The ports! He remembered his dictionary search. The Porta Marina was the way to the sea!

'We will go to the gate that leads to the sea,' Cy told Linus. He gave the younger boy an encouraging smile. 'You hold the whip,' he said. He hoped that giving Linus something to do might take his mind away from the situation a little.

'This way, then,' said Linus, pointing with the whip to the road Cy should take.

Hot cinders and fine ash were collecting in drifts against the doors of the shops and houses. Some of the rocks which the volcano had thrown out were so large and heavy that several buildings had collapsed. Ahead of them the road was blocked.

'We could try the road to the Forum Baths,' said Linus. 'We can follow it west and then cut through past the Forum and that way reach the gate to the sea.'

With great difficulty Cy turned the chariot round. The wheels churned in the thick layer of ash. The ground shook under them and with a great heave Vesuvius again belched flame and molten rock.

Linus covered his eyes with his hand. 'May the gods protect us,' he whispered.

Looting had begun. Smashed amphorae littered

the road. A group of rough men stood outside a wine shop and eyed the approaching chariot. As Cy drew even, one of the thieves who had been injured on the side of his face and was bleeding from the mouth tried to grab the horses' reins. The horses reared and plunged, hooves flailing the air.

Linus raised his whip and hit the man across the head. 'We should travel faster,' he told Cy. He leaned across and brought the lash down on the backs of the horses.

With terrified whinnies the horses leaped forwards and began to gallop at a furious pace. Cy clung on, trying to control the chariot as the wheels bounced off the cobbles and struck sparks from the road below.

Through the streets of Pompeii Cy raced for his life. Past the Temple of Jupiter and the north side of the Forum, horses and chariot clattered. Cy wrenched on the reins to swing them to the left. He could see the roof of the Temple of Apollo. Another twist in the road brought him close by the Basilica and now the Porta Marina was in sight!

The Porta Marina was one of the narrowest exits of the city. The two vaulted passageways, one for pedestrians and one for vehicles, were both clogged with traffic. Some people were trying to leave, others trying to gain entrance to the city.

Cy tried to warn them. 'Go to the sea!' he cried. 'Leave the city!'

'To the temples!' they shouted. 'Isis and Apollo will save us!'

In the crush of wagons and carts the horses shook their heads and began to stamp and kick wildly. Linus jumped out and soothed them as Cy guided them through. Then they were off down the slope and onto the main Roman highway.

The animals' fear drove them on. Linus gripped the sides of the chariot with both hands and Cy held grimly onto the reins. 'Do you know any way to reach the sea where there might be a boat?' he called to Rhea Silvia.

'Yes!' Rhea Silvia called back. 'When Linus and I were small the house slave took us to a little cove where the fishermen beached their boats. It is reached by a cliff top ... South! Take the road south, and I will watch out for the turn-off.'

On a rise beyond the town they turned to look at the scene behind them. The cone of Vesuvius was almost hidden by a dense mass of gas and pulverized rock. A blizzard of grey ash was falling on Pompeii and a great darkness was moving across the land.

Cy urged the horses on. 'Faster! Faster!' he cried. 'Here!' shouted Rhea Silvia. 'We turn here!'

Cy saw an unpaved road branching to the right and dragged the horses to a standstill. With Linus's help he managed to turn their heads and they set off down the lane at a fast trot. Soon the road disappeared into rough hilly terrain and he realized that they would have to get out and walk.

A hot sulphurous wind was howling through the olive trees scattered about the hillside. Wrapped in their cloaks with the wet cloths against their mouths, the refugees were almost doubled up against it.

'Can we rest?' asked Rhea Silvia.

'No,' said Cy. 'It will get worse. In a few hours there will be a hurricane which will destroy everything before it.'

In the distance, through the murk they could see the mountain of Vesuvius. From the centre of an enormous red and black cloud lightning arced, flashing silver and blinding white. The appearance of the boiling column of smoke was changing. It was condensing, beginning to drop . . .

'Hurry! Hurry!' cried Cy. 'You must get into a boat. Then the wind will blow you to safety.'

'I need to stop for a minute,' puffed the Dream Master.

Rhea Silvia and Linus stopped.

'Go on! Go on!' Cy cried to them.

They turned and kept climbing.

Cy took a few deep breaths and went to help the Dream Master. He grabbed the little man by both arms, hauled him to his feet and began to push him up the hill ahead of him. As he did so Cy looked up. Against the skyline he could just make out two figures. They were there! With her arm around her brother, Rhea Silvia had reached the top of the cliffs!

CHAPTER XIX

'Excuse me! Can I talk to you?'

Cy turned round. A small bespectacled figure in a pointed hat was running to catch him up.

'Wait!' Cy called after the Dream Master.

'What is it *now*?' the little man asked wearily.

Cy pointed at the boy, whose round glasses were falling off the end of his nose. 'He says his name is Larry Trotter and he knows the secret of Marzipan.'

The Dream Master reached up and rapped Cy

on the top of his head. 'You *do* get things confused in there, don't you?'

Cy turned back but the boy had disappeared and a large owl was sitting where he had been.

'Concentrate!' gasped the Dream Master. 'Don't lose this Storyline. Save *that* one for another Time.'

Cy thought really hard. The owl winked and was gone.

'When we get back I will take a long rest,' said the Dream Master. 'A *very* long rest.'

Cy thought for a minute. He held out his hand. 'If it would help at all, you can have my piece of dreamsilk,' he said.

'It has a force of its own,' said the Dream Master. 'I cannot control it.'

'Why not?'

'Don't you understand?'

There was a look on the Dream Master's face that Cy had not seen before. Regret? Pride?

'It is yours, Cy. It belongs to you.'

Linus and Rhea Silvia were waiting for them at the top of the cliff.

'I never thought that the sight of the sea would be so welcome,' said Rhea Silvia.

Cy looked down in the direction she was

pointing. Below and to the left he could see the Mediterranean. The water was troubled and moved in moody swirls at the base of the cliffs. But it was clear enough to make out, and . . .

Cy gripped Linus's arm. 'Do you see it?' he cried out. 'There is a boat!'

They squinted through the drifting fog. On the sand at the water's edge was a small boat of the kind used by the shell fishermen. Small enough for Linus and Rhea Silvia to sail, but large enough to take them far away from the shore and any danger.

Linus lay flat on the cliff edge. 'There is a path,' he said. 'A rough way worn down by goats, no doubt, but we will follow it.'

'I need to leave you here,' said Cy.

'We understand,' said Rhea Silvia. 'You must go and look for your sister.'

'Sister?' said Cy. 'Oh, yes.' He remembered that Linus and Rhea Silvia believed Lauren to be a slave in a villa outside the town.

'We will go to your country, to Britain.' Rhea Silvia put her arm around her brother. 'I would like to live in a land where there are no volcanoes.'

'What about your parents?' asked Cy.

'We will find them and tell them,' said Rhea Silvia.

Linus nodded.

It seemed that the parents of ancient Rome had little to do with their children, thought Cy. Or was it that the children grew up much more quickly?

Rhea Silvia spoke again. 'Cyrus, I declare that you are a free man.'

The three friends looked at each other. Cy felt his dream waver and was aware that the landscape was drifting. His piece of dreamsilk must be fading.

I have to leave them, Cy thought, and quickly. He knew that he should hurry if he was to take the Dream Master safely back to the twenty-first century to be reunited with his dreamcloak.

'We must say farewell,' said Cy sadly.

'We have a saying,' said Linus. '*Ave*. It means both "hail" and "farewell". I hope that, though we say farewell now, sometime we may again say hail to each other.'

'We too have a saying,' said Cy, 'which is almost the same. "See you later."'

'*Ave*.' Linus reached out until his fingers touched Cy's own. 'See you later.'

'*Ave*, Cyrus.' Rhea Silvia too stretched out her hand to Cy.

'*Ave*,' replied Cy.

CHAPTER XX

'Not bad,' said the Dream Master. 'Not bad at all.'

The Dream Master sat cross-legged on Cy's bed. He nodded in approval. 'You've brought us both back safely to your own TimeSpace. Everything is correct. Day. Date. Year. Place.'

With a feeling of great relief Cy sat down on the end of his bed. He unfurled his fingers from around his piece of dreamsilk. It lay quietly on the palm of his hand. 'Look,' he said to the Dream

Master. 'See how it has changed again. The edges are less ragged, it seems more, more . . . concentrated and complete.'

The Dream Master examined the dreamsilk without touching it. He raised his head and held Cy's gaze for a long moment. 'You have a powerful Imagination. You must learn to use it well.'

'The energy seems to flow *through* it,' said Cy. He held the dreamsilk up, and watched it ripple like waves on flat sand. 'But you cannot see where it goes, or where it comes from.'

The Dream Master shrugged. 'There are things that it is not given to us to understand.'

'Yet there must be a focus,' Cy persisted. 'A centre for this power.'

The Dream Master looked at Cy with eyes as wise as Time. 'For this piece of dreamsilk, it is you, Cy. *You* are the centre.'

Mrs Chalmers was really pleased with the class work on the volcano project. Basra had made a model using raspberry jam to show lava flowing down the hillside. Innis had researched more recent volcanic activity with scanned images of eruptions in Africa and Sicily. Vicky had decided she wanted to be a volcanologist. She had put together a career profile as part of her work, showing equipment used and fieldwork undertaken by men and women who worked right beside active volcanoes. Mrs Chalmers had commended Cy's work, his vivid 'eye-witness' description of a volcano exploding and his drawings of scientific experiments showing how volcanic eruptions take place. She had been particularly impressed with his collection of *dinarii*. When she asked him where he had obtained the little silver coins which showed the head of an ancient Roman emperor, Cy told her that his grampa had found them in Italy during the Second World War. He didn't think she'd believe him if he told her the truth, which was that he had picked them up from the sand in the Amphitheatre at Pompeii just before Vesuvius erupted.

School might *just* be a bit less boring than being at home, Cy decided as he walked home on the first day of the new term. Not that home was exactly *boring* at the moment . . .

To say that the Dream Master was upset when Cy unwrapped the dreamcloak was (and here Cy felt quite proud that he could use just as much alliteration as the little man) Undeniably an Understatement of an Utterance.

157

'I think I rescued it in time,' said Cy. 'It had only got as far as the water filling the drum of the washing machine.' Cy didn't mention that his mum had set the machine to 'boil wash'.

The Dream Master surveyed the gloppy mess. 'My dreamcloak,' he moaned. 'My beautiful dreamcloak.'

Cy held his breath, waiting for the explosion of bad temper, but it didn't happen. The little man seemed more dejected than angry.

'It will be all right, won't it?' Cy asked anxiously.

'It will take *aeons* before I can regenerate this again,' said the Dream Master. 'Is your mother mad?'

Cy didn't think his mother was mad. But she was certainly bewildered. At the weekend Dad and Lauren had returned from their shopping trip after only one hour.

'*One hour!*' said Cy's mum. 'You and Lauren agreed on a school skirt after only *one* hour?'

'No trouble at all,' said Cy's dad. 'The thing is not to make too much fuss, I think.'

Cy's mum stared at them both suspiciously. 'What exactly does this skirt look like?'

'It's absolutely fine,' said Cy's dad. 'I don't think

even *you* could object to the length.' He sat down in a chair, picked up the evening newspaper and, with a smug expression on his face, began to read.

'Oh, and by the way,' Cy's dad added, 'I had to buy her a new tie. She said something about giving the one you bought her to someone who really appreciated it.'

It wasn't until breakfast on the morning of the first day of school that Cy and his mum saw Lauren in her school uniform. Cy's mum had just bitten into a slice of toast when Lauren entered the kitchen. The new school skirt hung elegantly from Lauren's waist in soft pleated folds which reached almost to her ankles.

Cy's mum choked. Fine drops of marmalade sprayed out across the breakfast table. His dad leaned over and thumped her on the back. 'All right, dear?'

Eyes streaming, Cy's mum nodded.

Later, as he walked behind Lauren on his way to the bus stop, Cy noticed that his sister's skirt was split at the back, almost three quarters of the way up.

CHAPTER XXI

SPQR.

Mrs Chalmers herded her class into the antiquities section of the local museum. 'SPQR.' She pointed to the banner just inside the door. 'Can anyone tell me what that means?'

Basra had his hand up first. 'It's Latin, miss. It means the Senate and the People of Rome. They used it when the Roman Empire was a republic.'

'Well done!' said Mrs Chalmers. She introduced herself to the museum guide, who was waiting to

show them round. 'I've got the best class in the whole school here for you today.'

Cy's friends smiled at each other. That's what I like about Mrs Chalmers, thought Cy, she is always so positive and encouraging.

'There was a Roman settlement here from early times,' the guide began, 'and excavations have turned up a wide range of artefacts over quite a wide area. We have sandals, pottery, cooking utensils, jewellery, and just outside the town are remains of a bath house and barracks for soldiers.'

'But not gladiators?' asked Innis.

'You would have to go to Rome to see gladiators,' said the museum guide.

'Or Pompeii,' added Cy.

The museum guide nodded. 'Yes, I do believe that they had gladiatorial combats at Pompeii.'

'We have been studying volcanoes,' explained Mrs Chalmers, 'so my class know a bit about Pompeii, especially Cy.'

'The eruption which buried Pompeii was in AD seventy-nine,' said the guide. 'Some of these artefacts are from later than that. The Roman armies did not leave Britain until the fourth century, and many people from the Roman Empire never left. They settled and intermarried and could be our ancestors.'

Had Rhea Silvia and Linus managed to find Britain? Cy wondered as he followed after the guide. It would be a long and dangerous journey but one which they had both seemed determined to make. Cy felt sad that he would never know. A dream ended when a dream ended, according to the Dream Master, and Cy couldn't go back to that one and find out what had become of his friends. In fact he couldn't dream any of his own dreams until his Dream Master's dreamcloak had re-energized itself. And the Dream Master had forbidden him to use his own piece of dreamsilk until he'd done some more mind-training exercises.

'Cy, pay attention.' Mrs Chalmers nudged him.

'The soldiers of a legion had a practice of making an altar or erecting a statue wherever they settled. Sometimes these were portable, sometimes more permanent.' Their guide had stopped in front of an oblong stone carving which had been mounted on the back wall of the museum.

'This wall plaque was found in a field quite close to your own town. It is carved in relief – that is, the flat piece of stone has had a scene carved out of it. The figures and objects are therefore raised up above the surface.'

Cy and his classmates crowded round and looked to where the guide was pointing.

'The only information about this particular find is contained within the carving itself. We can find no reference to it nor anything of a similar type anywhere else.'

Cy looked up and blinked.

'If you look along the bottom you will see letters and the number VIII. You all probably know that the Roman numerals VIII mean the number eight. So we can therefore say that the Eighth Legion were involved here.'

Cy edged closer. There was something familiar about the carving. Had he seen it somewhere before? But the guide had said nothing like it had been found anywhere else. Still keeping his eyes on the carving, Cy turned his head to listen as she began to speak again.

'What is quite different about this is that there are only two figures represented here, and both are young people, a boy and a young woman. This could be a free Roman woman and her personal slave, or a boy with his nurse.'

Cy's eyes went from the figure of the boy to the girl and back again. He gasped.

'What do you think?' the guide asked him.

'I think . . .' Cy said slowly, his heart beginning to beat faster as he took in more details. 'I think . . . that they look more like brother and sister.'

'I never thought of that,' said the guide. She stepped back and put her head to one side. 'That is a very interesting idea.'

'Cy always has interesting ideas,' said Vicky.

'It could be that the girl represents some kind of minor goddess,' the guide went on. 'The Romans worshipped gods, goddesses and spirits of all kinds. They built both huge temples and small shrines to them. Every house would show reverence to the household gods by having their own *lararium*. It could be that the soldiers stationed here had a particular devotion to this young woman. This sculpture might be a depiction of a woodland sprite, for example.'

By now Cy had worked his way right to the front of the group. His heart was thumping fast in his chest and his eyes were glistening.

'The boy is drawing, and around his feet are scattered small cubes of stone known as *tesserae*,' the guide went on. 'These were used in different colours and sizes to make mosaics. It may be that he is designing an image of the goddess to decorate a wall or a floor.'

Cy gave a start. What had the guide just said? Cy peered more closely. Yes, those *were* pieces of mosaic scattered around the feet of the two figures. It must be them! Cy closed his eyelids for a moment in happiness. Rhea Silvia and Linus *had* arrived safely in Britain after all!

'There are three letters at the top, an R and an S close together and then an L. L is the Roman numeral for fifty—'

'No,' Cy interrupted. 'L is for Linus.'

'Could be.' The guide gave Cy a challenging glance. 'In that case, what would you say R and S stood for?'

'Rhea Silvia,' said Cy.

'*Silva* means "wood", so that would fit in quite well with my theory of the woodland sprite.' The guide looked very pleased.

'And Rhea Silvia was the mother of Romulus and Remus,' added Mrs Chalmers. 'You may just be right, Cy.'

Cy didn't say anything. His mind was now content. His friends had escaped from Pompeii and arrived in Britain. It looked as though they had become mosaic-makers, so well thought of, in fact, that a sculpture had been made of them. Or perhaps Linus had carved it? Cy remembered

Linus's drawing of the Dream Master and smiled to himself.

'There are letters and numerals along the base which have been partially decoded.' The guide traced the inscription with her finger. 'CUL, and then VIII, which are the Roman numerals for eight, and then the letter R. One could speculate that R stands for Rome. We have yet to decide finally what CUL means.'

'That could be an exercise for the class,' said Mrs Chalmers. 'When we get back to school we could all attempt to draw this carving and make up our own translation of what the letters mean.'

Cy's eye followed the line of text as Mrs Chalmers spoke. CUL VIIIR. If you did as the museum guide said and changed VIII to the Arabic number 8, then the inscription read CUL8R. Cy mouthed the message out loud, and then his jaw fell open. It was what he had said to Linus and Rhea Silvia as they parted. CUL8R – see you later!

'You will notice that the girl is wearing a kind of scarf.' The guide had begun speaking again. 'That also is uncommon. Boys would not have worn a toga until they were older, and women wore a garment known as the *stola* which covered them from head to foot. *Stola* is the origin of the English word "stole". Nowadays we don't use the word "stole" so much, we use "scarf" or "shawl" to describe a piece of material draped across the shoulders. In this carving the *stola* is very narrow and appears to be tapered. It almost looks like a modern tie but that can't be, as ties were not used until centuries later. I think it gives that appearance because of the way that the sculptor has fashioned the stone to depict the folds of the material.'

Cy felt a sudden prickling of the skin on the back of his neck. He stared hard at the statue. 'Excuse me,' he said. 'Do you think that the material has a pattern?'

The guide peered more closely.

'A stripe?' suggested Cy. 'Like a school tie?' Chloe and Eddie giggled. Cy ignored them.

'You know, it does look a bit like that,' the guide agreed.

Cy looked again at the two figures. Then he reached forward and, with the tips of his fingers, he touched the outstretched hands.

The guide noticed this and smiled at Cy. 'Our everyday custom of shaking hands has been passed down to us from two thousand years ago. When you met someone you stretched out your hand. It was to show that you were not reaching for your sword.'

'I remember,' said Cy under his breath.

'Then you would greet the person by saying, "*Ave.*" It is Latin and it can mean welcome or farewell.'

'*Ave*,' said Cy softly to the figures on the wall plaque. '*Ave*, Linus. *Ave*, Rhea Silvia.'

The class went on to the next exhibit and Cy began to turn away. Then he stopped and looked back quickly. Right on to the outside edge of his vision there was the briefest of movements. For a shaving of a second of Time it seemed to him that Rhea Silvia's and Linus's hands had reached out, and their fingers fluttered farewell.

But that was only his Imagination.

Wasn't it?

I am the
Dream Master.
My dreamcloak helps me
move through Time and
Space to give you the
dream that you want.
But there are rules –
rules that should not
be broken . . .

The DREAM MASTER

by Theresa Breslin

There are good dreams and there are rotten dreams, and once they're over, they're over. Or are they . . . ?

For one morning, as Cy is about to wake up from a terrific dream about Ancient Egypt, he discovers that he can get back into his dream world. There's just one problem: the Dream Master, who isn't used to stroppy boys standing up to him and wanting to break all the rules.

And as Cy moves back and forth between the present day and the land of the Pharaohs – sorting out all kinds of problems with schoolwork and bullies – dream life and real life become ingeniously intertwined!

Cy's enthralling first adventure with the Dream Master is available in Corgi Yearling paperback: ISBN 0 440 86382 1.

Cy is breaking all the rules. Chased by his furious Dream Master he zaps through the dreamcloak to really *live* his dreams, and it's Twenty Types of Trouble Double-Mixed when he ends up in a Pharaoh's tomb.

In Ancient Egypt the early Pharaohs were buried in huge pyramids in the desert and precious things placed inside to help them in the afterlife. But robbers broke in, so the later Pharaohs had secret tombs cut inside the rock in the Valley of the Kings. This is where a very uneasy Cy finds himself in Chapter Six of *The Dream Master*:

Cy rubbed the back of his neck. He had an odd feeling . . . as if there was someone else close by. He paused to look at some papyrus scrolls, and then, just behind him, he heard a soft creaking noise.

He whirled around. The sound was coming from inside the wooden mummy case standing upright in the corner . . .

DREAM MASTER NIGHTMARE!

BY THERESA BRESLIN

Every dream needs a master – someone in charge, just like someone telling a story. But when Cy has a go at running his own dream, things don't quite work out the way he wants. Suddenly Viking invaders are burning down a village, chasing after him with huge axes – and a bossy Saxon princess thinks he is a useless swineherd. His dream is out of control.

Only Cy can sort it out. It's *his* dream, *his* story. And if he fails, the bloodthirsty barbarians in his dream could burst through into real life . . .

Switch from now to then and back again in Cy's second hilarious adventure published in Corgi Yearling paperback: ISBN 0 440 86395 3.

On a school trip to research the Vikings Cy dreams up a story about Norse invaders. But then everything goes horribly wrong and bloodthirsty barbarians begin chasing after him with huge axes and threatening to burst through into Cy's real life. His dream has become a *Nightmare!*

Travelling in their swift longboats the Vikings made terrifying raids on our coasts. But they also traded and settled; many place names still have Viking connections. Here is a list of Viking words and their meanings:

Viking word:	Meaning:
by	a farmstead
toft	a homestead
thorpe	an outlying farm
ness	a headland
dale	a valley
kirk	a church

These words appear in lots of British place names, such as Inver**ness** and Der**by**. Look on a map – are there any near where you live? If so there might have been Vikings rampaging right through your own town at one time!

DREAM MASTER GLADIATOR

BY THERESA BRESLIN

In *Dream Master Gladiator* Cy and his Dream Master find themselves taking part in the gladiator games in Pompeii.

During Roman times gladiators fought in many different ways. Some used a sword and shield while others had a trident and a net. Often they had to fight wild animals as well as each other, just as Cy's Dream Master has to do battle with a lion in the amphitheatre in this adventure!

To help with his school project, in Chapter One of *Dream Master Gladiator*, Cy asks his Dream Master for some fast facts about volcanoes.

Here are five fast facts:

• There are about 500 volcanoes located all over the world.
• A huge volcanic eruption in 1500BC at Santorini is supposed to have started the legend of the lost city of Atlantis.
• Krakatoa was an island with an enormous volcano – most of the island disappeared when it erupted in 1883.
• When Mount St Helens in the USA exploded in 1980 it affected weather conditions around the world.
• A good website to check out information about volcanoes is one run by the University of North Dakota: http://volcano.und.nodak.edu/vw.html. There you can see photographs of volcanic eruptions that are currently taking place!

Dream Master Arabian Nights

by Theresa Breslin

Cy's powerful imagination means that he can zap through Time and Space to really *live* his dreams. But dreams aren't easy to control – even with the help of a crabby Dream Master!

So it's a Thousand and One Types of Trouble when Cy accidentally draws a famed Arabian princess into his world. Soon she's causing havoc, summoning terrifying creatures, and hurtling into Cy's school on her magical flying carpet. But there's even more trouble to come when the Princess learns that a TV talent competition is coming to town and she's determined to enter . . .

A terrific fantasy tale that explores the magic of storytelling all over the world. Published by Doubleday: ISBN 0 385 60425 4.